# BOSS RULES

## Boss #8

## VICTORIA QUINN

# CONTENTS

| | |
|---|---:|
| Chapter 1 | 1 |
| Chapter 2 | 23 |
| Chapter 3 | 45 |
| Chapter 4 | 57 |
| Chapter 5 | 75 |
| Chapter 6 | 95 |
| Chapter 7 | 115 |
| Chapter 8 | 127 |
| Chapter 9 | 165 |
| Chapter 10 | 187 |
| Chapter 11 | 211 |
| Chapter 12 | 251 |
| Also by Victoria Quinn | 261 |

**Hartwick Publishing**
**Boss Rules**

# CHAPTER ONE

Titan

"How was your day?"

Diesel stepped out of the elevator with his tie already undone. It hung around his neck, one side slightly longer than the other. Fatigue was in his eyes, but the second he looked at me, that handsome smile came into his face. "Doesn't matter. Your day is the only one that matters." His muscular arms circled my waist and cradled me against him, his powerful chest pressing up against me just like a solid brick wall.

"Not true."

He pressed his warm mouth against mine, his lips teasing me. "True."

"It was boring. I watched reruns of *I Love Lucy*."

"That sounds like a great day. Took all your medication?"

I rolled my eyes. "Like I would ever forget. I'm pretty much addicted to those painkillers."

He moved his lips to my forehead and pressed a soft kiss against my skin. His scruff rubbed against me slightly, scratching me every time he moved. His fingers were much gentler than they used to be. Now that I carried a wound in my chest, he handled me as carefully as possible.

I missed the old days.

"You still haven't told me about your day." My fingers moved to the buttons of his collared shirt, and I undid each one slowly.

"I worked."

I rolled my eyes. "I figured that much. What else?"

"And I worried about you."

"That was a waste of time because I'm perfectly fine."

"You're perfect," he said. "But not perfectly fine." He kissed my cheek before he stepped away. "I'm going to shower. You better be naked and ready when I get out." He turned his back as he walked away, commanding the room as he passed through it.

I'd missed that side of him.

After he got in the shower, the front doors of the elevator opened again and revealed Thorn. He stood with his hands in the pockets of his slacks, his navy blue suit complementing his bright eyes. Thorn had an appearance that qualified him to be a model, and he was perfectly aware of that. I hoped he wouldn't waste that potential with a life of loneliness. "You're looking good." He stepped into the penthouse and walked up to me in the living room. He examined my face as well as my arms, looking for signs of healthy life. His eyes never undressed my body, not even when we were engaged. Diesel was the only man who had done that—and made it obvious. "But a little thin…"

"My medication kills my appetite."

"You never had an appetite before, so it must be pretty strong," he teased.

"Diesel isn't happy about it. When I'm better, he says he's going to stuff me like a pig."

"I second that." He smiled then took a seat on the couch. "Is he here?"

"In the shower."

Thorn rested his elbows on his knees and rubbed his palms together.

"You want a drink?"

"No, thanks," he blurted. "Sit."

Both of my eyebrows shot up. "Excuse me?"

He hid his flustered expression as well as he could, but it wasn't good enough. "This is serious. I'm not sure if I should tell you this now or when Diesel is in the room."

Now that I understood this wasn't just a casual visit, I sat beside him. Tension radiated off Thorn in waves, the kind that pierced through the skin like a hot summer day. I crossed my legs and regarded him with a stoic expression. Anytime I was in the face of adversity, I remained calm and accepted whatever would come to pass. Even when a gun was pointed at my face, I kept the same level of control. "Everything alright?"

"Yeah, I think so. I just had an interesting visitor at your office today…"

After Bruce acted on his vendetta against me, suspicious characters were alarming to me. I was a careful and paranoid person, but now I took suspicions even more seriously. "Who?"

"A woman. Should I wait for Diesel?"

I shared every aspect of my life with that man. I hadn't married him yet, but my commitment to him was ironclad. There were no secrets, no lies. I'd completely opened up my world to him. "He's been having nightmares lately…about me being shot. We talked about it and he seems to be better, but he's not back to himself just yet either."

Thorn continued to rub his palms back and forth, sliding his skin across skin. "Then what do you want to do?"

"I don't know… I don't want to lie to him. But I don't want him to stop going to work either."

Thorn waited for me to reach a response on my own.

No matter how many times I considered it, the answer didn't come to me. "Just tell me, and I'll think about telling him."

"Alright." He leaned back against the couch and rested his hands on his thighs. "This woman stopped by the office asking about you. She wanted to know why it was taking so long for you to recover. She was visibly upset, extremely concerned. She was acting like she knew you…like you were close. She said she'd been out of the country during the shooting and didn't hear the news until a few days ago."

I heard everything he said, but I didn't know what to make of it. "Her name?"

"Bridget Creed. You know her?"

I shook my head. "Never heard of her…"

"That's alarming. Because she obviously knows you."

"If she did, she would have called me or emailed directly."

"True. But the way she acted…I can't explain it. If I'd told her you died, I know she would have sobbed right then and there."

For a complete stranger to care about me that much and show up at my office was… I wasn't sure what it was. "Maybe she's a fan? Who's a little obsessive?"

"It's possible. I asked how she knew you two times—and she never answered."

"Because she doesn't know me."

"Yeah…" Thorn's voice trailed away as he stared into the distance. Judging by the way he pulled himself away from me, something was bothering him. He hadn't said everything he needed to say.

"What is it, Thorn?"

"I'm probably just being paranoid…"

"Tell me." Diesel was bound to finish his shower any minute. It didn't take him long to dry off because he didn't need a hair dryer and he usually shaved in the morning.

"Well…she had brown hair, she was thin, had green eyes and…she looked just like you."

"Looked like me?"

"Her cheekbones go high the way yours do. Her eyes are shaped the same way. And her figure…she has long legs like you do. Like I said, I'm probably just being paranoid and drawing conclusions over stupid things, but I'd be lying if I said I didn't notice it."

"Thorn, what are you implying?" I wanted him to be perfectly direct because I was getting specific ideas in my head.

"Maybe she's your mom…" Thorn turned back to me, his gaze taking in my features like a sponge soaking up water. "I realize it's a little ridiculous, but unless your mom lives under a rock, there's no way she doesn't know you're Tatum Titan, you know? You never changed your name. No matter what her reasons were for giving you up, she would have made the connection."

I never felt incomplete not having a mother in my life. My father did well enough, and he gave me plenty of love to make up for a missing parent. Sometimes my mind would wander and I imagined what she looked like, but my thoughts didn't continue that way for long. She didn't want me in her life, so I didn't think about her at all.

Thorn kept staring at me. "Titan?"

"I'm thinking."

"I know your features like the back of my hand because you've been in my life for so long. She reminded me of you the second she walked in the door, even before she said anything. It could just be a coincidence...but I thought it was strange."

"It probably is just a coincidence."

Thorn turned quiet, his palms coming together again. "Are you going to mention this to Diesel?"

"I don't know..."

"The woman didn't seem like a threat. Like I said, she just seemed concerned."

"What was her name again?"

"Bridget Creed," he answered. "I did some research but didn't find much. She's been married for the last ten years to a software developer. He does pretty well, but they aren't rich by our standards. She has two sons with him. I couldn't trace her life further back than that. At least, I didn't have time. This just happened like an hour ago."

If she really was my mother, all I had to do was hire someone to trace her past. Her name would be in the hospital records from when she gave birth to me. There would be a marriage license. Unless she changed her name before she got married, it would be all the evidence I needed.

"Are you going to dig?"

I knew getting my answer wouldn't change anything. Whether she was my mother or not, it didn't change the past. It didn't change the future either. She'd made her choice, and I respected that decision. But that didn't mean I was required to care about her. "No."

"Really?"

"Even if she is my mother, it wouldn't change anything."

"I guess…maybe you should talk to Diesel about it."

"I'll think about it…"

Thorn stared at me, obviously distressed about our conversation. "Should I not have said anything?"

"No." I grabbed his arm and gave him a gentle squeeze. "You did the right thing. Thank you."

"I felt like I should. I would want to know."

Thorn would never know what he would want. He was born into a loving family with parents who adored him. He'd always been complete that way, and that was perfectly fine. But he never knew what it was like to be the child of a single parent. Things were more difficult, like money and stability. I would never insult my father's memory by saying his care wasn't good enough. It certainly was. I wouldn't be the strong woman I was now without him.

Diesel came out of the bedroom in just his black

sweatpants. His torso was wide and thick with muscle, and his tanned skin was kissed with grooves where the slabs of muscles were separated. He was built like a soldier, the definition of a strong man. I was lucky I got to see him walk around my house like that every single day. "What's up, Thorn?"

"Hey, man." Thorn immediately rose to his feet, knowing he'd just dropped a heavy conversation on me. "I just stopped by to check on Titan."

Diesel walked up to him and shook his hand.

Thorn did the same, always treating Diesel with respect now that he'd been vindicated.

"She's getting stronger every day," Diesel said. "I'm excited to have her back to normal. She's kinda like a glass vase right now. I'm worried I might shatter her."

I rolled my eyes as I stood up. "I'm not a vase."

There were a few drops still on his chest, spots he'd missed. They got buried in the cracks of his muscular frame. "What's going on with Ms. Alexander? Is that still happening?"

Thorn and I hadn't even talked about it.

Thorn smoothed it over without making it obvious that we forgot to even mention it. "Are you free tomorrow?"

"Thorn, I'm free every day," I snapped.

Diesel's eyes narrowed. "I was under the impression Thorn was handling all of this?"

I knew he was about to unleash his fire all over me. "He is. But I need to meet the woman before I consider a partnership with her. It would be ridiculous not to."

"I agree," Diesel said. "But we agreed you wouldn't be working right now."

"It's not really working," I argued. "She would just stop by the penthouse."

Thorn took a step back, doing his best to disappear from the conversation.

"It is working," Diesel snapped. "It can wait until you're ready to return to work."

"That's ridiculous," I countered. "Thorn is doing everything for me, but he can't make this judgment call entirely on his own. Besides, I'm pretty restless cooped up in here. I would like some company. She'll be here for an hour at the most."

Diesel crossed his arms over his chest.

Thorn turned to the TV even though it wasn't on.

"This is happening." I wanted to join my life with Diesel's in every way imaginable, but I didn't want him to make all my decisions for me. Sometimes his advice was sound, but sometimes he overstepped his boundaries.

He narrowed his eyes further.

"I'm sorry, Diesel," I said. "But life goes on."

Diesel stepped back, all the muscles in his body thickening in annoyance. "I'm not happy about this."

"Yeah, I can tell," I said sarcastically.

Diesel stepped away from the conversation, silently excusing himself. He took his hostility with him, but we could still feel it surrounding us. It infected the air, entering our lungs with every breath.

"Are you sure about this?" Thorn asked when Diesel was out of earshot.

"Ignore him."

"It's easy for me to do that," he said. "But it's not so easy for you."

I was used to having that big caveman around the house all the time. I understood his moods, his protectiveness. Everything he did came from love, so that was why I excused his possessiveness. But I knew I had to stand my ground—and he would respect me for it.

———

A few hours after dinner, his anger finally started to fade away.

Diesel sat beside me on the couch, his arm moving around my shoulders. The cushion dipped noticeably because of his weight. A game was on the TV, but his eyes were on me. The hard lines of his face were similar to an outcropping of a mountain. Jagged in some places and smooth in others, his expression was a beautiful landscape.

"I'm glad you finally came around."

"I just want you to get better as quickly as possible."

"The worst is over," I said gently. "You forget how much progress I've made. Now that I've gotten this far, nothing is going to hold me back." My fingers moved to his chin, and I felt the thick stubble that had grown in since he'd shaved that morning. The shadow highlighted the contours of his face. I liked to touch him every-where, but his chin was particularly beautiful to me. When I wasn't allowed to have him, I fantasized about doing this very thing. When we sat across from each other at my desk, I could feel the pressure in my finger-tips just by imagining it. "You forget how strong I am."

"Never. I just forget how weak I am."

"You aren't weak, Diesel." He was the strongest man I'd ever known. Whenever he was beside me, I felt his presence protect me. I never needed a man to provide me security, but I enjoyed his. It made me feel more powerful than I already was because I had the love of the most powerful man in the world.

"When it comes to you, I turn irrational. When it comes to you, I can't see straight. I get emotional… I change. It's not a reflection of all I am…but a product of my ridiculous love for you." He turned his face into my hand and kissed my fingertips.

"I'm lucky that I'm the woman who gets to turn you irrational."

A slow smile crept into his lips, and he gently pulled me tighter against him. "You always know what to say."

"That's because I know you so well."

He rubbed his nose against mine, giving me a soft touch he never shared with anyone else. He could be aggressive with me, just as he was with the women before me. But that softness was something he reserved for me. "I'll let this go. Having her stop by for an hour or two shouldn't be a big deal."

"It's not a big deal at all."

"But you're in a place of vulnerability. You're at home because you're injured. It's not the same as someone coming into your office while you sit behind your desk. They can see all your power standing on the top floor of your building. It's different when the setting is here."

"I don't think that'll be an issue. No matter where I am, my power is unmistakable. I have a strong reputation, and she realizes that. Just because I'm willing to form a partnership with her doesn't mean I'm willing to do anything to make it happen. She's a smart woman. She knows not to cross me."

His large fingers moved into my hair, gently massaging the strands. When I stayed home all day, I watched the clock and counted down the hours until he came home. But I knew if I were busy at work, I'd be doing the same thing anyway. My work was just as important to me as it'd always been, but now Diesel gave me something else to be passionate about. "Thorn seems to be doing a great job taking care of things for you."

"He really has."

"Maybe you should ask him to do it again when you're on maternity leave."

Now we were jumping into the future. "I'm sure I can work until the day I give birth."

"You definitely can't walk in stilettos all day long like you're used to."

"Well, of course. But I think I'll be fine."

"And after the baby comes?" he pressed.

"I'll have a nanny help me out."

Judging by the frown on his face, he didn't like that. "I don't want a stranger taking care of my kid."

"We'll vet them extensively before we allow them to care for our child. And I'll be there most of the time. But we don't need to worry about that right now. We have a lot of other things to take care of." The idea of having a daughter made me think of what Thorn said. He suspected the woman who stopped by my office was my mother. She had me, but she chose to leave. I couldn't imagine myself doing the same thing. I wanted to be a mother, to grow my own family. The desire had nothing to do with my mother's abandonment. It was just something that would give me the most joy.

Diesel must have noticed my expression fall because he said, "What is it, baby?"

I didn't want to keep Thorn's tale a secret. Whether Thorn's suspicion was right or wrong, I couldn't hide it from Diesel. We planned to share our lives together, which meant we had to share everything else. "Thorn said a woman stopped by my office today asking about me. She was worried about my health after the shooting. She seemed legitimately upset about it…and she looked just like me."

Diesel's expression didn't change at first. Slowly, it morphed into a stone-like mask. He was guarded, concerned, and hard.

"Her name is Bridget Creed. Thorn looked her up and said she's been married for the last ten years, and she has two sons. That's all he knows, but he didn't look deeper." I didn't need to spell out the words because Diesel had already reached the same conclusion.

His fingers pulled away from my hair, and he released a quiet sigh. "What do you think?"

"I don't think anything."

"You think it's her?"

I knew exactly what he was asking. "Whether it is or not, it doesn't matter."

Diesel questioned me with his look. His features only changed slightly, but it was enough for me to understand what he was thinking.

"She chose to leave. I accept her decision and don't think less of her for it. She couldn't handle the responsibility of being a mother, so she left me with my father, who did an amazing job. If she didn't want to be there, I didn't want her to be there. But she can't walk back into my life now, even if she does really care. She gave up that right the second she walked out on me. She can't have it both ways."

Diesel's expression softened. "That makes sense. But

don't you want to know if it's her? I can make a quick phone call, and we can get to the bottom of it."

Like I said, it didn't change anything. "I don't want to know."

"Are you sure? If it were me, I'd want that answer."

"But you aren't me, Diesel." I dismissed the conversation by turning away. "Thorn said she didn't seem dangerous. I don't think there's anything to worry about."

"But she might try to talk to you. Maybe you should be prepared."

"I still don't want to know, Diesel." I grabbed the remote and turned up the volume on the TV, ending the conversation by drowning out the silence with cheering fans.

Diesel finally dropped it. His fingers moved into my hair again, slowly caressing me. "Who do you think is gonna win, baby?"

———

It'd been weeks since I wore a dress and heels.

It felt right.

I missed dressing up like I had somewhere important to be. I missed having a reason to get ready in the morning. The only purpose I had lately was saying goodbye to Diesel when he left for work.

The rest of the time, my life had no meaning.

But now the pumps felt perfect on my feet. They

were a little painful—as they should be. My dress wasn't as tight because I dropped a few pounds during my illness, but it still fit me well. I styled my hair in soft curls and applied my makeup heavier than I used to.

I imagined we would conduct our meeting in my living room. It seemed unnecessary to take her all the way down the hallway to my private office. We already had ambitions to work together, so it seemed pointless to play games.

The light over the elevator lit up once someone stepped inside from the lobby.

I knew it was Thorn and Ms. Alexander.

I smoothed out the front of my dress and approached the elevator, my heels clapping against the hardwood floor. My hands came together in front of my waist, and I listened to the distant grind of the elevator as it slowly approached the top floor.

The light lit up again before the doors opened.

Thorn stood in a gray suit with a coral tie. The light colors complemented his fair features. His dirty-blond hair was perfectly styled, and his light blue eyes looked like a spring afternoon.

Ms. Alexander stood beside him in a pencil skirt and a buttoned jacket. She had jet-black hair, tanned skin, and a face pretty enough for a picture. She wore a cute pair of heels, but her height was still considerably less than Thorn's. She was shorter than me as well.

I smiled when we made eye contact.

Thorn extended his arm, having her exit first. Then

he stepped into my living room and greeted me with a hug. "You cleaned up good."

I hugged him back. "Thanks."

He winked before he stepped away. "Titan, this is Ms. Alexander. I'm excited the two of you are finally in the same room together."

Ms. Alexander held herself with perfect grace. With a straight spine, poised shoulders, and a beautiful smile, she extended her hand to shake mine. "It's truly an honor, Ms. Titan. I've followed your career for a long time. Without strong women like you to pave the way, I wouldn't have the opportunities I have today."

A lot of people blew smoke up my ass to get what they wanted. They didn't realize flattery was useless on confident people. But in her case, it seemed genuine. I was an excellent judge of character, and based on my research and her appearance, she seemed like the real deal. "That's nice of you to say, Ms. Alexander. I appreciate your flexibility coming to my home this afternoon. I'm still not well enough to return to the office just yet."

"It's no problem," she said. "I'm happy to be here."

Thorn eyed us back and forth while his hands rested in his pockets.

"Let's take a seat." I indicated to the couches in the living room before I sat down on the long sofa. I made sure I left a spot for Thorn so he could sit beside me.

Ms. Alexander sat on the couch across from me.

And Thorn sat beside her.

I hid my surprise well, but I still wasn't prepared for

his actions. Did that mean anything? Or had staying home for so long messed with the cogs in my head? "I understand Thorn has been the mutual messenger during our discussions. He's done a great job handling my companies during my leave, and I can't thank him enough. But I'm glad we're having this conversation face-to-face."

"Me too." She crossed her legs and rested her hands in her lap. Just as I was poised, she didn't seem nervous at our interaction. She held her own very well. "Thorn has been a wonderful mediator. Bringing us together was a great executive decision. We both have contributions we can make to this idea. Together, I think we can make an energy company that will rival anyone who opposes us. You have the experience to turn this technology into a brand, and I have the knowledge to make the technology forever evolving. No one else will be able to copy us because by the time they catch up to my last design, I will have two more products on the roadmap. We can make a great team."

Ms. Alexander was a scientific genius, and she didn't doubt her abilities. I liked her confidence, and I liked that she got straight to the point.

Thorn spoke next. "Ms. Alexander is looking for an equal partnership. You both have distinct strengths that could be deadly when they're combined together. It'll allow each of you to work on the things that interest you most. I've gotten to know each of you separately, and you're both the most extraordinary businesspeople I've interacted with. I truly believe you'll make the perfect team."

Ms. Alexander gave him a gentle smile, the kind that reached her eyes.

I smiled too, but my eyes were on her.

"So, let's do the most difficult part," Thorn said. "Percentages."

I already knew what I wanted. "Sixty-forty. The reason being, I'll be investing a great deal of my money and resources into making this technology a global phenomenon. I have all the right contacts, the branding power, and the expertise. This will allow Ms. Alexander to focus on her work exclusively."

Thorn immediately shifted his eyes to Ms. Alexander, predicting she would have an immediate response.

"It needs to be fifty-fifty," she said politely. "I understand your reasoning, and in most situations, it would make sense. But when we handle this kind of technology, I want to be part of the decision-making. I want to make sure my inventions are being used in a way I agree with. If we do it your way, then you're simply buying me out. I really want to work with you because I know we'll do great things, and I also respect you, so I'm not trying to be difficult or greedy. For me, it's not about money. It's about involvement. It's about partnership."

She could be pulling a number on me, but I believed in her sincerity. I'd put a ridiculous offer on the table to buy her out, and she didn't blink an eye over it.

Everyone cared about money, but perhaps she didn't care as much as most people did.

"It's important for me to make an impact on the world. I don't want to be forgotten in your shadow, Ms. Titan. I want to be viewed as an equal contributor. I want the world to see two smart women working together and making a difference. It's my legacy—and that's the most important thing to me."

I held her gaze as I considered what she said. My investment in solar energy had already done very well, but it was bound to die out without her new innovations. I was used to doing everything on my own, but in this sector, it wasn't possible. I needed someone with the right scientific background—and she was the best in the business.

I could argue back and forth to get what I wanted, but I suspected it wouldn't change the end result. Moving forward, I would be relying on her input most of the time anyway. She understood the technology far better than I did. "Fifty-fifty."

She immediately smiled.

"Fifty-fifty of this new company we'll merge together. It has no effect on any other institution I own, even if it's a conflict of interest. Those are my final terms." I didn't foresee a conflict of interest at that moment, but I didn't know what would happen in the next twenty years. I could invest in a competitor's product if I wished.

She could argue against that, but she already had a

great offer on the table. She asked for the sundae she wanted, and it would be risky to push for a banana split instead. My fierce reputation preceded me, and people didn't make the mistake of misinterpreting my niceness for weakness. If I compromised, it was suicidal to push for more.

But Ms. Alexander made the right decision. "We have a deal."

# CHAPTER TWO

THORN

Once the meeting was finished, I returned to the office a few blocks over. Autumn went back to her complex on the other side of the city, and we parted as business partners rather than lovers.

I'd been at the office for a few hours and had just finished a meeting with Titan's assistants when Titan called. She called straight to my cell and bypassed her own employees.

She and I hadn't discussed the meeting with Autumn yet, and I knew that was the subject of the conversation. "Hey, I think that went well."

"I agree. She's a smart woman."

I knew Titan could read people with surprising accuracy. She didn't take long to break down someone's character, even in a short conversation. She picked up on subtle clues, like body language and confidence levels. She'd always known who Diesel truly was, despite the evidence that stacked against him. I thought her heart had overruled her logic, but I'd been wrong. I should have trusted her instinct. "Extremely."

"I'm not thrilled by the even divide we agreed on, but I understand why she asked for it. I would have done the same thing."

When it came to business, I needed to have absolute control. I liked to make all the decisions without having to answer to someone else. That also carried into my personal life as well. "This is a special circumstance. In most cases, the person you're doing business with can't compete with your resources. But since you're working in the science space, you're at a disadvantage. Autumn has a lot of power because she's the only one with the brains to produce the resource."

"Autumn?"

I swallowed the lump in my throat when I realized my error. I shouldn't have addressed her that way, not when it implied we had a personal relationship. I didn't even call Titan by her first name. "She asked me to call her that."

Titan didn't comment on it, but her suspicion was heavy in the silence. "You're right. She does have a lot of power."

"But she seems genuine about it. If all she cared about were getting ahead, she would have taken your initial offer. I think this will be a great setup for both of you. Together, you'll make billions."

"I'm sure you're right, Thorn. I'm eager to get back to work and get started."

"Don't push Diesel," I teased. "He seemed pretty ticked the other day."

"He's always ticked. Ignore him."

"If that were true, you wouldn't be marrying him."

She sidestepped the comment. "You guys should get started without me. There's a lot of groundwork to do, but you know how I like things."

"I'll give you daily reports through email."

"Okay, thanks. Ms. Alexander needs to lay out all of her projects so we can determine exactly what direction we're going in. Depending on what she has in stock, it could determine our branding moves."

"We?" I asked. "I thought you weren't involved in this?"

"I think I can be involved remotely."

"What about Diesel?"

She sighed. "Don't worry about him. He'll get over it. Sitting here doing nothing is stressing me out more than just working."

I believed that. Titan was a goal-oriented person. She needed to be doing something in order to be fulfilled. Once she accomplished a task, she was ready for the next. The constant drive never stopped, but it gave her life a comfortable speed. "Did you tell him about Bridget?"

Her long pause was my answer.

"How did he feel about it?"

"He didn't say much. He offered to dig into her and confirm her identity. I said no."

I respected Titan's decision and agreed with it.

"I told him I wanted to forget about it and move on."

"Have you been thinking about it much?" If I suspected my long-lost mother were trying to come back into my life, I'd obsess over it. I'd want to know everything about her, to look at her in person and see the genetic resemblance between us.

"No." Her response was cold, but also genuine. "It makes no difference if Bridget is really my mother or not. She's not a part of my life, and I don't want her to be. I don't hold any anger toward her. But I respected her decision to abandon me and move on with her life. Therefore, she needs to respect my decision to abandon her."

As cold as Titan's response was, there was undeniable truth and logic in it. Titan didn't get worked up about a lot of things. She was pragmatic, allowing herself to assess a situation with complete objectivity.

But would she be so objective if she looked the woman in the eye?

The woman who looked just like her?

Maybe that situation would never present itself.

But what if it did?

"I should get back to work."

"Of course," Titan said. "Thank you, Thorn. I

know you're putting in a lot of hours to help me out. I'll compensate you when I return to work."

"I don't want compensation, Titan. That's not what this is about."

"I know. But I'm giving it to you anyway. Call me if you need anything." Click.

———

My day didn't end until eight that evening. I finished everything at the office, handled my own projects, and then went to the gym. There were days when skipping my workout was tempting, but it was one obligation I couldn't abandon.

Not if I wanted to stay in such good shape.

I got out of the shower, sat on the couch, and texted Autumn. *Thinking of you.*

The three dots popped up instantly. *What a coincidence. I'm thinking of you.*

I wanted to invite her to my place, but that would be rude. It was dark outside, and she shouldn't be out and about by herself. I didn't know if she had a private driver or not. *How about I swing by?* I didn't have a clue where she lived, but it was probably in a nice penthouse like mine. She didn't have my kind of money, but she was still exceptionally wealthy.

*You don't strike me as the kind of man who asks a question like that.*

I smiled at her playful banter. I was trying to be

somewhat polite, but maybe she didn't like polite. *Give me your address. And get ready for a good fuck.*

*Now that sounds more like it.*

I changed then got into the back seat of my driver's car. He took me a few miles away, to an area that was filled with narrow townhouses. They were on the upscale side of town, and once I stopped in front of her house, I saw blooming flowers despite the harshness of winter. The yard was perfect because someone must take care of it often.

I walked up the stairs to the front door and rang the doorbell.

The door opened a moment later, revealing Autumn standing in a see-through black dress. The top pushed her tits together, and the fabric was so thin I could see the curves of her body perfectly. I could see the diamond in her belly button and the lace of her thong.

I pushed the door closed behind me without taking my eyes off her. The polite thing to do would be to look at her place and give her a compliment.

But I didn't give a damn about being polite.

My hands moved to her hips, and my mouth pressed against hers. Her petite frame was yanked against mine, and the kiss that ensued burst with sparks. I sucked hard with my lips because I couldn't get enough of her. My tongue danced with hers, making up for the harshness I just extended.

My hands slid down her body until I gripped her perky ass, her toned muscles luscious as hell. One of the last things she said to me in private was that she only wanted me, not Connor. The thought made my dick thicken another centimeter, at least.

I guided her backward until I entered her living room. Instead of taking the time to find her bedroom, I settled for the large sofa in her Pottery Barn look-alike living room. The thin dress was pulled over her head, revealing her naked tits. With hard nipples and flushed skin, she looked desperate for a deep fuck. Her jet-black hair was aching for my fist.

I ended our kiss so I could watch my fingertips glide down her smooth skin. I felt her shoulders and her slender arms then streaked down her tits that were as tight as her ass, and moved down her belly. My forefinger touched the diamond hanging from her navel, and then I reached the lace of her black panties.

I licked my lips automatically, my entire body hot at the idea of fucking her. The surprise she gave me when I opened the door made this clandestine meeting even sexier. I'd never seen a woman look so perfect, so real.

My cock was as hard as steel.

She reached for my jeans and loosened them as she looked up at me. She bit her bottom lip then released it, letting her lip flick up. Her breathing intensified, and the longer she didn't kiss me, the more intense the moment became.

I listened to the zipper move down.

I heard the button snap open.

I watched her eyes narrow as she pushed down my jeans and boxers.

My dick pulsed for her, greeting her with a profound twitch.

She licked her lips.

Damn.

She pushed my bottoms to my knees then pulled my long-sleeve over my head. When I was naked for her to appreciate, she touched me the same way I'd just touched her. She glided her fingers over my naked body, lightly stroking the defined areas of muscle as she sank lower.

She moved down my abs and slowly approached my cock.

Finally, her fingers gently touched my length, her warmth making my cock twitch instinctively.

Damn, it felt good.

Her other hand moved to my balls, and she gently massaged the most tender area of my body with her long fingernails. Her other hand pumped my dick and smeared my own lubrication down my length.

I kept my eyes focused on her, but my strength was starting to fade away. The instant my dick was in her hands, I lost all my power. All forethought evaporated. All I could think about was sticking my dick in every hole she possessed.

I dipped my fingers underneath her panties and found her clit. It was covered in arousal, and she was so slick my fingers slid all over her folds. It seemed like she was slathered in an entire bottle of lube—except she produced it all on her own.

And she did it because of me.

I didn't need to prime her for my big dick. I needed to give her twenty minutes of foreplay to ensure she would come. She was ready for me even before I arrived on her doorstep.

I pulled my hand out of her panties and stared at the stickiness between my fingertips. When I stretched my fingers apart, the substance stretched too. I felt the slickness on my skin before I sucked everything off.

Her eyes smoldered, and her lips parted once more.

I wanted to feel her lubrication with my dick, not my fingertips. I wanted to sink into that warm and wet pussy until I was balls deep. I wanted to feel her bare walls, feel her constrict around me more intimately. "My papers are in my pocket." I'd stopped by my usual clinic before I went to work. "Yours?"

"On the kitchen table."

I was clean, and I was sure she was too. I didn't want to halt the moment to read the results myself. If she had something to tell me, she would say it. And I'd be rolling on a condom right now if my results were anything but unremarkable.

"How do you want it?" I'd give her whatever she asked for. It didn't make a difference to me what the position was because I would enjoy it regardless. But I was her slave, the man she wanted to use over and over.

She urged me onto the couch and I sat down, my frame resting against the cushions.

She straddled my hips and sat on my lap, my dick rubbing against her cheeks. With her hands secured to my shoulders, she guided herself up and forward, her eyes on me.

I pointed my dick at her entrance then pulled her down my length.

There were no words to describe what I felt.

Just perfect pussy.

I rolled my head back and gritted my teeth as the sigh of satisfaction swallowed me whole. I'd been bareback with women before, but it was never like this. She had the tightest and slickest pussy in the entire world.

My hips gripped her hips, and I pulled her tighter against me, filling her completely.

She lost her breath and flinched, my long length and thick size hurting her slightly. She breathed through the pain and focused on the pleasure. She bit her bottom lip in this sexy little way, and then she started to move up and down.

Fuck, I'd have to make her come quick.

Because I wasn't going to last long.

———

She freshened herself up in the bathroom, and I pulled on my boxers before I sat on the couch again. I should have put the rest of my clothes on, but I was too drained to move. We started fucking on the couch and then moved to the rug on the hardwood floor. The fire was strong when we began, but it was simmering coals by the time we were done.

I was covered with sweat.

She was full of come.

I'd been in arrangements with women before, and being that focused on someone was beautiful in its own way. I didn't think about work, other women, or any of the shit going on in my life. I just fucked and enjoyed it.

With Autumn, it was different.

The connection was stronger.

With her, it was like there wasn't even a world outside the front door.

It was just the two of us.

While I waited for her to return, I looked around her townhouse. The living room was filled with gray sofas on a white rug. It contrasted against the dark hardwood floors. A few paintings were on the walls, images of flowers along a riverbed. Her stone fireplace complemented the rest of the room, the white stones accenting her light furniture. The TV wasn't on, but being in her room brought me a profound sense of peace.

It was cozy.

She returned minutes later, her body wrapped in a cotton towel. Her hair was dry and her makeup was the same, so she'd just washed the sweat off. She glanced at my clothes on the ground then stared at me on her sofa. "I thought you'd be gone already."

The sight of her just in a towel was as erotic as the lingerie she wore earlier. "No, that's you." She was the one who liked to slip out the second the opportunity presented itself. She took hit-it-and-quit-it to a higher level. I didn't stick around for long either, but I at least waited for the woman to get out of the shower.

She sat beside me and crossed her legs. There were a few drops of moisture on her tanned skin, and I pictured kissing them away. I wanted to trail kisses down her spine and taste the water as it rolled down her back. My arm moved around her shoulders, and I pulled her beside me so we could both look at the dying fire.

"Your house is really comfortable."

"Thanks." She rested her cheek against my shoulder. "I considered moving in to a place like yours, but I like having a yard. It's nice to see flowers all the time."

"And your fireplace is cool. You don't see those too often."

"They're perfect for the wintertime. So warm."

I rested my cheek against her head, snuggled up with her on the couch. I liked having her next to me even if my dick wasn't getting anything out of it. She was so soft. And she smelled like summer even in the middle of winter.

Now I didn't want to move. I continued to watch the fire dwindle until it was just hot ash in the fireplace. Bright spots of orange and red burned because they were still so warm. Every once in a while, a gentle pop would fill the air. "The meeting went well today."

"I think it did too. Titan is an incredible person."

"Why do you say that?" She hadn't shown any extraordinary behavior that afternoon.

"She was shot just a few weeks ago, but she looks like she could run a marathon."

"She's just putting up a front," I said. "She's still combating the pain."

"Regardless, that's not easy to do. People think they'll be strong when tragedy strikes. But when it really comes down to it, the fear will get to them. Titan seems to be the exact same person she was before."

I would never get the lobby footage out of my head, the way she stared down her attacker without showing fear. Then she pulled that badass stunt and got the gun from him even though she'd been shot. She pulled that trigger and won the war. "She's the strongest person I know. She's been through a lot, but there's not a single tragedy that will hold her back. She pushes on even when the odds seem hopeless. When people question her ability, she smiles then proves them wrong. That woman is fearless, and she's a role model to us all." I viewed her highly in a lot of respects, as a friend and business partner. She started off under my direction, but she bypassed me a long time ago. "She grew up with nothing, so that gave her a survival instinct. That instinct has gotten her where she is today. She'll never forget what it was like to be hungry, homeless, and afraid. That's why she never takes anything for granted."

Despite the comfortable position we were in, Autumn moved out of my embrace. She scooted to the other side of the couch and severed our contact completely. She still wore the satisfied look in her eyes, so it didn't seem like she was angry about anything. But something felt a little off. "I'm excited to work with her."

"You should be. Titan will take you far."

She turned her gaze to the fire, her black hair obscuring half her face.

"You want me to throw on another log?"

"Let it die out," she whispered. "I'm going to bed soon anyway."

I grabbed her by the ankle and dragged her leg to my thigh. I pulled the other one as well and situated her feet on my legs. Then I gave her a foot massage, gently digging into the muscles she crammed inside stilettos every day.

"You don't have to do that…" She brushed off the advance, but she had a noticeable softness in her voice, like she was already slipping off into sleep.

"I want to." I loved her small feet. She had a sexy arch, pretty toenails, and the softest skin I'd ever felt. I enjoyed feeling the balls of her feet directly against my chest when I pounded into her unbelievable pussy. I loved seeing these small feet rock heels like they were flats. I loved everything about her, from her plump lips to her painted toenails.

She rested her head against the armrest with her

arms still keeping the towel around her. She was right when she said it was getting late. It was almost ten in the evening. I had to be up at the crack of dawn to get ready for work the following day. She probably did too.

But that wasn't enough to make me leave.

"Titan said we should get started. There're some things we need to go over."

Her eyes grew heavy-lidded as I continued to massage her. "When?"

"Tomorrow."

"I have availability tomorrow. Just let me know what time."

"How about one?" I watched my thumbs press into the arch of her foot.

"Sure."

This was the first time I'd ever rubbed someone's feet. Sometimes my fingers gently touched a woman's back when she lay beside me in bed, but that never lasted long. Now I was going out of my way to make this woman feel good—without getting anything out of it. "I want to ask you something."

"If you keep rubbing my feet like that, you can ask me anything you want."

I smiled then moved my hands up to her toned calves. "Did you want to fuck me because of my big dick?"

Her eyes were closed when I asked the question, but a huge smile stretched across her face. "Oh god…" She resisted the urge to laugh, but a few chuckles came out. "Did you really just ask that?"

"I'm serious. You were totally cold to me until you saw my boner in my slacks."

She ran her hands through her hair, but the smile didn't fade away.

"When have you ever been embarrassed to say the truth?"

"Never," she said. "Your question is just very crass."

"I'm a crass man. Now answer me."

"Come on, Thorn. I thought you were hot the second you walked through the door. I've always thought you were sexy."

I'd never grinned so wide in my entire life. My cheeks actually felt strained because I spent most of my time wearing the same no-bullshit look. "You've always thought I was sexy? What does that mean?"

She opened her eyes and propped herself up so she was sitting higher. Her embarrassment was slowly fading away, but she was still slightly flushed in the cheeks. "You're a famous guy. I've seen you in the news for years."

Some of that news was good, but most of it was bad. At least she still thought I was hot. "Good to know. So was my dick the turning point for you?"

"I admit I was impressed when I saw it. Can't say I've been with a man who compares."

Damn right.

"And it feels as good as it looks…"

My hands paused as they gripped her slender feet. She showered me with the kind of compliments that were dangerous to my ego. Her input wasn't brand-new information because I already knew what I offered women. But coming from a hot little number like her, it made me feel like a king. "I'm glad you like it."

"So to answer your question, yes. I guess I just wanted that D."

I grinned. "And I'm more than happy to deliver."

"When did you know you wanted me?" she asked.

I rolled my eyes. "Don't be stupid."

"Excuse me?"

"You know when I wanted you." My enormous bulge was as effective as a billboard.

"But was it because of something I said?"

"No. It was from everything. From the way you dress, to your gorgeous curves, your perfect complexion…and your success. You're a genius in a field where the population of women is less than ten percent. You rose on your own merit, and now you provide for your parents. You're down-to-earth because of your humble beginnings, but you never let your achievements inflate your ego. You aren't arrogant, but kind and straightforward. You're a badass woman who stands on her own two feet."

She listened to every word I said, but instead of smiling, she kept the same expression.

"Everything about you makes you sexy as hell, your beauty and your brains." I'd just paid her a compliment that any woman would appreciate, but it didn't seem to have any effect on her at all, like she didn't want to hear it.

"I guess you have a type."

My fingers continued to rub her feet, but I didn't focus on my actions anymore. "A type?"

"Yeah, the strong and successful woman type."

I'd never screwed another woman like her before. None of the others fit any specific criteria. I just found them sexy, and I wanted to screw them. For men, we didn't need a lot of qualifications before we fucked someone. "I don't really have a type…" My fingers dug into her tight muscles, and I felt the tiny knots underneath the skin. If I pushed the right way, I could unroll the fascia sitting underneath the skin.

"Titan."

I turned back to her, hearing the name but not understanding the meaning. "What?"

"Titan," she repeated. "She fits into that category perfectly…and you were going to marry her."

For a second, I didn't have a clue what she was talking about. But then the lie returned to me, the façade I played out for a year of my life. The entire world believed I dated Titan for the last year and proposed to her. For some reason, I didn't think that lie existed when I was with Autumn.

I wanted to tell her it was all bullshit, but now that she was working with Titan, I couldn't correct her assumption. It didn't matter anyway, so I just let it go.

Whether she thought I actually dated Titan or not, it didn't change our arrangement. "Yeah, I guess."

The time had passed quickly since I started rubbing her feet, and now it was almost eleven. I should be getting ready to go, but even now, I still didn't want to leave. If she invited me down the hall to her bedroom to sleep over, I would take her up on her offer immediately. But I knew she would never invite me. "As much as I love your feet, I should get going."

"I should get to bed too." She got off the couch with the towel still wrapped around her chest, her dark hair falling down her back. She walked to the front door, her small feet tapping against the hardwood floor as she moved.

I pulled on my clothes then followed behind her, moving slowly on purpose because I didn't want to leave. If I were at home right now, I'd already be in bed. But being with her gave me a new jolt of energy. She was like a shot of caffeine.

I stopped in front of the door and resisted the urge to yank her towel off. I wanted to swoop her into my arms, take her to her bedroom, fuck her into the mattress, and then sleep with my dick still inside her. "Can I ask you something before I go?" My hands rested on her hips, and I stepped closer to her, watching her eyes soften in reaction.

"Sure."

"Connor Suede."

She stared at my lips before her eyes flicked up to mine. "Interesting question."

"You never wanted him? You seem attracted to him."

"He'd just offered me something incredible. Of course, I was happy around him."

"What did he offer you?"

"The same thing he offered to Titan, a spotlight. But a spotlight that concentrates on the beauty and success of a powerful woman. It's the kind of image I want. It's the kind of publicity I crave. He's going to design the perfect clothes for me to convey that image. It's a pretty big deal, and I'm incredibly flattered."

Her explanation made sense. "That makes me feel better."

She smiled at me. "For not wanting a relationship, you get really jealous."

"I'm not jealous."

"You don't want me to be attracted to other men. You don't think that's a little ridiculous?" She pulled her towel higher up her body, her smile accompanied by a look of amusement.

"I told you I'm just possessive."

"Same thing, Thorn."

"I don't agree."

"Well, I know I get jealous. But at least I have the balls to admit it."

My gut instinct was to smile at her confession because the idea of her being jealous inflated my ego even more. "Jealous of what?" I hadn't even looked at another woman since the first time I met Autumn. She'd been the only woman in my mind—and in my bed.

She opened the front door to let me out. "Good night, Thorn." She hid behind the door so the cold wouldn't hit her bare skin.

Before I crossed the threshold, I circled my arm around her waist, and I leaned down to kiss her.

She kissed me back, greedy as usual.

I ended the embrace but kept my face close to hers. Her eyelashes were the same color as her dark hair, and that darkness made her eyes stand out even more. My fingers squeezed the towel at the small of her back, and I pressed a kiss to the corner of her mouth. "Yes, I get jealous…really fucking jealous."

# CHAPTER THREE

Vincent

It was seven in the morning, and I was standing outside the MET in my suit and tie. The sun was out and it was a clear day.

But it was cold as hell.

People passed on the sidewalk, going to work with a cup of coffee in their hand. Puddles were on the sidewalk, leftover from the thawed snow. I pulled back my sleeve and looked at the time.

I hoped she was still coming.

A cab pulled up to the sidewalk, and Scarlet emerged in red heels and a long-sleeved black sweater dress. An olive green scarf hung around her throat, and her brown hair was in large curls. Big sunglasses covered her eyes, but her smile couldn't be diminished by anything.

She walked toward me, looking like another model

in the city. She pulled off her glasses before she reached me and placed them in her purse. "Good morning, Vincent."

"Good morning, Scarlet."

She stopped in front of me, her hand resting on the strap of her bag. She didn't try to shake my hand, and she didn't try to hug me.

I didn't touch her either. A part of me wanted to, but another part wanted to put a thousand miles in between us. I stared at the perfect complexion of her face, the redness of her lips, and the brightness of her green eyes. My eyes lingered on the freckle on her cheek before I finally turned away. "This way."

"What are we doing here, Vincent?"

The guard opened the front door and ushered us inside.

I let Scarlet go first before I joined her. My driver appeared with two paper cups of coffee and handed them over.

"Coffee?" I extended the cup to her.

"Sure...thank you." She held it in her hand and took a drink. "How did you know I like soy lattes?"

"I called your assistant." I walked forward into the grand entryway, seeing the enormous room filled with ancient art pieces and sculptures. Everything from the Byzantine Empire to Mesopotamia was included in this historic museum.

She walked beside me, staring at me with a dumbfounded expression. "That was very nice of you, Vincent."

"Think nothing of it." I approached the first painting, a huge fresco that depicted one of the earlier wars in human civilization.

Instead of looking at the painting, she glanced around the room. "Are they open yet?"

"No. We're the only ones here." I didn't take my eyes off the image, seeing the exquisite piece of work right in front of me. It was thousands of years old. Generations had come and gone, and now everything they'd ever known had disappeared into the earth. Now I got to appreciate it with a hot cup of coffee in my hand, wearing a suit that was worth as much as a down payment on a car. These people had struggled in a way I would never understand.

"We have this whole place to ourselves?" she asked incredulously.

"I'm not a big fan of crowds."

"Wow…" She finally looked at the masterpiece on the wall. "Thank you for giving me the honor."

I stepped away and looked at the next piece.

"You like art?"

"I appreciate it. I'm not an expert by any means."

"I like paintings and sculptures, but I don't know much about history. Just a little here and there…"

We moved on to the next piece, standing side by side and never touching. We sipped our coffees as we enjoyed the silence of the expansive museum. They could play music overhead, but the silence was a lot more powerful. "Art can tell a lot about history even if you don't know what's going on. In the beginning, artists painted what they saw. So you see a realistic interpretation of life at that time. The colors aren't vibrant or romantic. They're simple, drab, and unremarkable. If you go into a modern art gallery to decorate your home, you won't see colors like this. You'll see bright bursts of color. As history goes on, the colors get bigger and brighter."

Scarlet took her eyes off the painting and looked at me. "I never knew that."

We moved through the museum, taking our time in one section. We both had work to go to in an hour, but I thought experiencing the quietness of the museum before opening hours would be a nice start to the day.

We enjoyed our coffees as we proceeded through the pieces, making small talk about what we saw. It was easy to talk about something that had nothing to do with either one of us. We talked about an artist's work and dissected its meaning. Scarlet had original insights and lovely opinions. I felt like I got to know her in a different way.

After a while, it felt more relaxed.

In this situation, we didn't have to talk about each other. I didn't have to talk about my late wife or wonder what happened with her and her ex-husband. This was a simpler way to spend time together, to do something that wasn't so heavy.

At the end of the hour, we left the museum and returned to the sidewalk. A line was already forming at the entrance, all the tourists waiting to see something we'd just enjoyed exclusively.

"Thank you for that, Vincent. That was an experience I won't take for granted."

"You're welcome, Scarlet."

Right on cue, my driver pulled up in my car. It was black with tinted windows.

"I'll give you a ride to work."

"That's sweet of you, but don't worry about it," she said. "I'm more than happy to take a cab."

I opened the back door. "I don't mind. Please get in."

She smiled before she got inside.

I got into the seat beside her, and my driver took us to her building. It was on the way, so it wasn't inconvenient. But even if it were, I wouldn't have cared. My phone buzzed in my pocket with endless emails, but I ignored them. Scarlet and I weren't making conversation, but I still didn't want to stare at my phone.

"That was really wonderful, Vincent. Thank you for taking me."

"Of course. How's the article coming along?"

"I'm almost finished…and it's wonderful. I think you'll like it."

"Great."

"Will you be able to come in for some photos tomorrow?" she asked.

"Sure. What time?"

"One?"

"I'll be there."

"That's great."

The car pulled up to her building, and my driver helped her out of her side of the car.

I got out and stepped onto the sidewalk even though I didn't know how to say goodbye. A handshake would just be weird at this point.

She held her bag and gave me a slight nod. "I'll see you tomorrow, Vincent. Thanks again."

"See you tomorrow." I kept my hands in my pockets so my body language was easy to decipher. I wanted to spend time with her, but I didn't want to touch her. I didn't want her to touch me either.

She waved before she walked away.

I waited until she was inside the building before I got into the back seat. I stared out the window as my car pulled away, unsure what I was doing.

I didn't have a clue.

———

I didn't know how long this would take, but I cleared my schedule for the rest of the afternoon so I wouldn't have to rush to another meeting. I walked into the building in the suit I'd been wearing to work, black with a pink tie. I checked in at the front desk and was immediately escorted to a different floor.

I stepped out of the elevator and was guided to the photography set. Backdrops and lighting were ready, and the photographer was making final adjustments. Scarlet stood at the clothes rack, sorting through the different selection of suits. When she was concentrating on her work, her expressions were harder than normal. But when her lips were pursed like that, she looked cute.

Did I just say cute?

Her hair was straight and pulled over one shoulder. She was in a bright pink dress with a gray scarf. Gray pumps were on her feet, and golden bracelets encircled her wrist.

I stepped inside without anyone noticing me and took advantage of the moment to stare at her.

She pushed through each outfit, her lips moving as she counted silently. When she finished the task, she stepped away from the rack and looked up. She nearly did a double take when she realized I'd been standing there for a while. "Hello, Vincent. Thanks for coming." She walked up to me but kept five feet in between us. Her hands came together at her waist, and she held herself professionally in front of her crew. It didn't seem like we'd had coffee together yesterday morning and walked through a hallway of ancient paintings.

My eyes were on hers, seeing the brightness of her eyes as it contrasted against the lovely colors she wore. Her makeup was different that day, her eyes smokier. As the editor in chief of the magazine, she obviously thought it was a requirement to look as good as the models.

I thought she looked better than the models.

I never found aging quite so beautiful as when I looked at her. Gravity had taken its toll and her skin wasn't as tight as Alessia's was, but like a fine wine, she got better with age. There was no doubt she had been exceptionally beautiful in her prime. As time passed, beauty naturally declined. But as a society, we shouldn't think that way. Our appearance changed, but not in a bad way.

I realized I hadn't said anything for the past minute, ignoring her polite greeting because I chose to stare at her instead. If we were alone together, it probably wouldn't have mattered. She knew I wasn't big on talking.

But we weren't alone. "I'm very happy to be here. Shall we begin?"

"Yes." She moved back to the rack and selected the first piece. "I know you have places to be."

I was free for the rest of the day, but I didn't tell her that.

She handed me the first suit, a deep navy blue with a smooth fabric that didn't possess the appearance of silk. It was stiff and well made, but it had a special touch against my fingertips. "Put this on, and we'll begin."

The photoshoot was held entirely on the floor with different backgrounds and changes in lighting. Scarlet's original idea was to take these photos in an exotic place, but she obviously had selected a different look.

She focused on the suit more than the background.

She stood behind the photographer and yielded the direction to him. She watched with her arms crossed over her chest, and sometimes she smiled when I changed my pose. Her eyes were glued to me the entire time. She could have stepped away and attended to the other tasks that were probably sitting on her desk, but she chose to stick around.

After two hours, we were finally done. I put my suit back on and felt the noticeable weight difference in the fabric.

Perhaps I'd have to buy some of those suits for myself.

The photographer cleared the space, and I met Scarlet by the door. She was placing every suit in a special plastic bag, protecting the fabric from the dust that filtered through the central ventilation system.

I eyed my watch before I walked up to her. "I hope the photos turned out well."

"Oh, they did," she said with confidence. "I saw them on the screen as Tony was working. They're beautiful. I can already picture the spread in the magazine. And I think I might put you on the cover."

"I'm not sure if I'm cover material."

"Oh, you are, Vincent." She smiled then zipped up the final bag. "The designer wants you to keep these as a thank you. I'll have them sent to your office."

"That's generous. Thank you."

"It's not that generous," she said with a chuckle. "If the world sees you wear these, it's great advertising—great *free* advertising."

No one else flattered me as much as she did. But her compliments seemed genuine, not hollow because she wanted something. My eyes focused on her movements, staring at her without restraint. Her motions were mesmerizing. The way her eyelashes flicked as she shifted her gaze was hypnotic.

She lifted her gaze up to me again, a soft smile on her lips. "I'll walk you out."

"Unnecessary. I'm sure you're busy."

"Then let me walk you to the elevator." She went first, passing through the door and into the hallway.

It was the perfect opportunity to look at her, but I didn't.

She walked me to the elevator then hit the button on the wall. "I'll send everything over once I have it. I want you to see it for yourself."

"Thank you." I adjusted a cuff link before I slid both hands into my pockets.

She stared up at me, keeping her professional stance even though it was just the two of us standing there. She kept her hands in front of her, her fingers locked together. Her shoulders were back, and her neck was straight. Despite her calm appearance, I could tell she was nervous around me. "Have a good afternoon,

Vincent." She smiled at me before she stepped away, her heels clapping against the tile.

Without preemptive thought, I felt my hand shake as it ached to grab her as she stepped away. I had to control myself and keep my hands to myself. Touching her was inappropriate, especially while we stood inside the *Platform* building. I got her attention with my voice instead. "Have dinner with me tonight." I hadn't planned on asking her to do anything, but watching her walk away filled me with dread. I didn't like it when we parted ways. She brought me a sense of comfort no one else could replicate.

She turned back to me, her eyes reflecting the same excitement that Times Square held on New Year's Eve. She had a natural smile that was easy for her to show, but she went the extra mile whenever I said the right thing. Without telling me how she felt, I knew she wanted to see me as much as I wanted to see her. "Just tell me when and where."

# CHAPTER FOUR

DIESEL

"What's up?" Brett walked into my office with a package under his arm.

I glanced up from my laptop. "Just working."

"Bullshit. We both know you don't work." He grinned before he fell into the chair facing my desk. "How's your lady?"

My lady. I liked that. "She's doing well. Gets stronger every day."

"I've been waiting for her to kill you, honestly."

"Why?"

"She must be going crazy staying at home all the time. And if you're her only company..." He shook his head. "That's gotta be brutal."

I grabbed the pen off the desk and considered throwing it right in his eye. "You gotta death wish today, Brett?"

"I just like pissing you off."

"So yes?" I teased.

He set the box on my desk. It was wrapped in black paper with a black bow.

I eyed it without touching it. It wasn't my birthday or Christmas, so I didn't know what it was for. I cocked an eyebrow and asked the question silently.

"It's for Titan. I think she'll like it."

"What is it?" I took it in my hands before I placed it off to the side.

"Luxury driving gloves. Made of premium leather from my favorite Italian designer, they'll be perfect when she hits the open road again. I also had her new last name etched into the material."

It was a thoughtful gift, so I felt like an ass for being annoyed by it.

"What?" Brett picked up on my mood.

"You know how I feel about reckless driving…"

"Titan isn't a reckless driver. She's always in control of her destiny. She just got herself out of a difficult situation and lived to tell the tale. You don't need to worry about that with her."

"And it might make her more anxious."

"She's gotta get better sometime. Now she has something to look forward to."

"And the last name…not sure about that."

"What do you mean?"

"We haven't decided if she's taking my last name or not."

Brett chuckled like it was a joke. "I can't see you giving her a choice in the matter."

"I don't want to give her a choice…but you know how she is."

"Not a pushover?" he asked. "I thought that was why you liked her."

"*Love* her," I corrected him. "And it is…I just don't want that to apply to me."

He chuckled. "Of course you don't…"

I would like her to take my last name, but I understood why she would be apprehensive about it. All of her life's work was tied to her last name. Even Thorn called her Titan on a daily basis. Not only were her businesses tied to that name, but it was also an essential part of her identity.

Could I really ask her to change all of that for me?

When we had kids, they weren't taking her last name. That was something I wouldn't compromise on. She wouldn't want to have a different last name from her kids, so that wasn't something she would enjoy.

It would be a difficult conversation, but one that was necessary. "How are things with Vincent?"

He shrugged and took a long pause before he responded. "Better. With such a dramatic change like this, it'll take time before it begins to feel normal. But he asks me to lunch once a week, and we talk about cars and sports…nothing too heavy."

"That's good." When Brett had walked into that restaurant to join us for dinner for our engagement celebration, I knew everything would be okay. Brett was a lot more forgiving than he let on. "I'm glad to hear that."

"I don't think I'll ever see him as a dad, but…"

"You can still be family."

"Yeah, I guess." He shrugged again. "I think Mom would want that, you know?"

I nodded. "Definitely."

"And he seems genuine about starting over. He's not the kind of man that apologizes just for the sake of doing it…"

"He's not." My father rarely apologized, so if he did, he meant it.

Brett adjusted his leather jacket before he rose to his feet. "Let me know if Titan likes the gift."

"Why don't you give it to her yourself?"

"I don't want to bother her." He walked up to my desk and gave me a fist bump. "When she's better, we need to have that engagement dinner."

"We will. I know she'll get excited about it."

He gave me a thumbs-up before he left my office.

Less than two minutes passed before Thorn called my cell.

I answered immediately, knowing he might have something important to say. He was running an empire that would jointly belong to me shortly, and he had an intimate relationship with the woman I loved. I would always share her heart with him, but I was okay with that. "What's up?"

"She told you about Bridget?" he asked bluntly.

"Yeah." It'd been a few days since we last spoke about it. Titan was clearly uncomfortable with the subject, and she shut it down the second she finished telling me about it. She wanted to bury it and move on.

"The woman looked just like her, man." He sighed into the phone. "It's her."

"You think so?"

"It was like looking at Titan in the future…"

I stared at my computer screen without reading the email I was halfway finished with. The brightness of the screen irritated my eyes, so I shut the laptop. "She doesn't want to know."

"Yeah, I picked up on that."

"She also said she didn't seem dangerous."

"I don't think she is. She seemed like a mother concerned about her daughter. This isn't another Bruce Carol nightmare…" His tone naturally dipped the second the man was mentioned.

Better not be. I'd never laid a hand on a woman, but I'd rip her apart if she was a threat to my future wife. "She says she doesn't want to know if it's her mother because it doesn't change anything. Doesn't want her in her life regardless. But I want to know…for myself."

"I'm curious too."

I glanced at my top drawer, where the information sat in a manila folder. I'd had my private investigator track down all the information so I could get my answer. Titan didn't want to confront the situation, but I needed to know. "Do you want to know?"

Thorn was quiet over the line, absorbing the powerful words I just said. "You figured it out?"

"I had my guy dig."

"Did he find something?"

"Does that mean you want to know?" Once I answered him, we would both be part of a secret Titan wasn't privy to. It was her business, but we were both butting in.

Thorn sighed over the line. "Yeah, I want to know."

I didn't need to open the folder again to see the answer. "It is."

Another sigh filled my ears as Thorn processed my answer. "I knew it…"

"Yeah." My investigator had dropped off the information that morning. I didn't hesitate before I ripped the packaging and took a peek inside. Maybe it was wrong for me to pry into Titan's life, but I couldn't just sweep it under the rug the way Titan did. I knew Titan was set on her decision, but she couldn't remain ignorant forever. If Bridget showed up again, I wanted to know everything about her.

"Fuck…are you going to tell her?"

"I don't know yet."

"She might get mad if she knows you kept it from her."

"I'm not keeping anything from her. She doesn't want to know, but I can't stay in the dark with her. If this woman tried to contact her once, she might do it again. I need to know everything so I can be prepared for it."

"Makes sense."

I couldn't anticipate the way Titan would feel once she knew the truth. Her mother abandoned her twenty-five years ago, and now she'd walked into her office like she had the right to inquire about her well-being.

She'd given up that right almost three decades ago.

"That's crazy," Thorn said after a minute of silence. "I never thought that woman would walk back into Titan's life. Maybe she wants money. Her daughter is a billionaire."

"It's possible. Her husband makes a pretty good living and she's a housewife, but they're nowhere near Titan's caliber."

"Then I'll keep my eyes peeled for her."

"Alright."

Jessica spoke through the intercom to Thorn, and I could hear her voice over the line. "Ms. Alexander is here."

"Thanks," Thorn said to her before he returned to me. "I've gotta go, Diesel. Thanks for keeping me in the loop."

"No problem. Quick question before you go."

"Yeah?"

"What do you think of Ms. Alexander?"

"What do you mean?" he asked, turning serious.

"I mean exactly what I said. You think she's the right partner for Titan?"

"Not a doubt in my mind, man. I think Ms. Alexander and Titan are going to be two peas in a pod. They're so much alike it's disturbing."

"And she's a trustworthy person?"

"Do you ever really know?" he countered. "But I'm willing to bet she is."

"Alright, thanks. I'll let you go."

"Talk to you later." He hung up.

I set my phone down then got back to work.

———

When I stepped inside the penthouse, it smelled like dinner. A fragrant aroma filled the air, smelling of pot roast and fresh carrots. Titan usually had dinner ready when I came by, but since she'd been injured, I'd been the one taking care of our dinner plans. "Something smells good."

She came out of the kitchen in jeans and a black button-up blouse. Her hair was done, makeup was on her face, and she wore a smile. "Your favorite."

"Are you talking about dinner or you?"

She moved into my chest and wrapped her arms around my neck. She greeted me with a kiss that she never shared with anyone else. It wasn't the kind of embrace she used to give me when we were just fucking. It was full of longing, love, and just a splash of lust. Her fingers moved slightly into my hair, and she gave me some of her tongue.

Great way to be greeted after a long day at the office.

I squeezed her hips but then forced myself to let go, knowing I couldn't handle her in any way that wasn't utterly delicate.

She pulled away, that model-like smile on her lips. "Missed you."

"Missed you." Sometimes I couldn't believe I got to come home to this every day. I couldn't believe this incredible woman was waiting for me, missing me while I was gone all day. My fantasies about women used to be only about sex. I never imagined a life like this. But now it was a dream I'd never even hoped for, and that made it so much more valuable. "I thought I was in charge of making dinner."

"I can handle it. It gives me something to do."

"How are you feeling?"

"I feel great."

"Excited for tomorrow?" We had an appointment with her doctor. They were going to take a look at her wound and determine if she was ready to remove the stitches that had been inserted almost a month ago. So far, her recovery had been uneventful—in a good way.

"You have no idea. If he doesn't take these stitches out, I'll do it myself."

"I wish I knew you were joking."

She smiled before she turned away. "You know I'm never joking."

I stripped off my jacket and hung it over the back of the couch. Then I removed my tie and opened the top button of my collared shirt. "I saw Brett today."

She spoke to me from the kitchen. "You did? How is he?" She carried the dinner plates to the dining room and set up everything for our meal. Then she retrieved the pot roast along with the silverware.

"Good. Things are going well with my dad."

"That makes me happy." She brought a bottle of wine and poured me a glass.

"You don't need to do that, baby." She still couldn't drink, so I refrained from doing it around her.

"It won't be much longer, Diesel. I'm fine."

I set the gift on the table. "He wanted me to give this to you."

"A gift?" She smiled as she sat down and picked it up. "I wonder what it is…"

I sat across from her and dished the pot roast onto my plate. The beef was tender and covered in a delectable sauce. Potatoes, carrots, and mushrooms were included. She made a side of broccoli that was sautéed in olive oil.

She ripped open the gift wrap then looked inside the box. "Wow…these are nice." She pulled out the black leather gloves and examined them under the light of the chandelier. "This stitching is incredible." She examined the name on the side, and instead of growing disappointed, she smiled. "That was thoughtful of him."

I nodded to the card. "Looks like there's a note."

She picked it up and read it out loud. "Sis, these are made for a badass, and you're definitely a badass…" Her eyes softened as she read the letter again, this time, in silence. Her eyes shifted back and forth as she took in the message. "Aww…that's really sweet."

"He's a good guy."

"He's a sweetheart." She folded the note and set everything off to the side.

"He's never bought me anything except a lap dance, so you should feel special."

Her eyes narrowed, immediately jealous.

I shrugged, unable to keep the smile off my face. "Long before you, baby."

She turned to the pot roast and scooped the food onto her plate. "How was your day?"

"Good." I thought about my conversation with Thorn but didn't mention it. "I've been thinking about our wedding plans."

"Yeah? I thought men didn't think about that sort of thing."

"Well, I do."

She smiled. "I'm a lucky lady."

"You want to do a quick courthouse thing?"

She made a disgusted face. "Uh, no. I've always wanted to get married outside."

"So you want a big wedding?"

"No. I want fewer than twenty people to be there."

"Good. Me too."

"Let's do it on a beach somewhere," she said. "I love Thailand. How about there?"

"It is a beautiful place."

"And we can start the honeymoon right away."

I grinned. "I do like the sound of that."

"I'm getting old, so I need to put my ovaries to use while they're still functioning."

Other men might be put off by that, but I certainly wasn't. "You want me to knock you up right away?"

She pushed her food around on her plate, her eyes watching her movements. "Depends. How do you feel about that?"

"Whatever you want, I'm in."

"Yes, I know," she said with a chuckle. "But what do *you* want?"

"I've always wanted a family. You know that."

"So you want to start now?"

"Sure. I know you're almost thirty-one, so you'd be thirty-two by the time the baby got here. Then we'd want to have another…so, yeah. We should get started."

"Wow, that was easy," she said with a chuckle. "I thought I would have to talk you into it more."

"Nope. I'm excited to get you pregnant. I'm excited to be a dad. I'm excited for all of it."

"Even though we won't have much time alone together?" she asked. "Everything has moved so fast, you know?"

"We have our whole lives, baby. Besides, our love will grow. I'm not worried about it."

"Great." She finally took a bite. "Then I'm excited."

"I'm excited too." I was thirty-five years old, fifteen years older than when my father had me. I wanted to still be young when they were adults. If I waited too long, I might not have the energy to run around with them. "Which brings me to my next point…"

"Why does that sound ominous?" she asked, taking a bite of broccoli.

"Because we're going to argue."

"I thought you liked it when we argued?" she teased.

"In certain contexts…"

"Tell me what you're thinking, Diesel."

I'd already imagined the conversation before it even started. She would fight me every step of the way. She would give me her reasons, and while they were legitimate, it wouldn't bring us closer to a solution. "Your last name."

She stared at me after she heard me speak. Then she turned her attention back to her food, eating like she hadn't heard me at all.

I knew she was gathering her thoughts, considering how to respond to me. "I guess we'll have to come to an agreement about this…" The response was vague, but it told me exactly what her stance was on the matter.

"You know what I want."

"Yes."

"So, we can argue in endless circles about it, or we could come to a compromise."

"I don't think I can change my last name, Diesel…" She stopped eating and set her fork down. She'd hardly eaten her food, but that was how her eating habits always were. I'd given up trying to push her to eat more. "It's my identity. It's my father's legacy. If I had a brother, it would be different. But I don't…"

"I understand, baby. I'd be open-minded to it if it were just the two of us…but it's not gonna be the two of us much longer."

"I know," she whispered.

"My children will have my last name." I didn't want to be harsh, especially when those tactics didn't work on a woman like her. But I wasn't going to compromise on this. "And I'm not doing a Titan-Hunt hyphen. Some people do that, but the second name always gets dropped. And even if it was Hunt-Titan, it still doesn't sound great."

"I think Hunt-Titan is the best compromise we're going to find."

I took a deep breath, steadying my anger the best I could. She was injured and recovering, and I shouldn't get her worked up right now. Her blood pressure would go up, and she would get upset. That wasn't good for either of us. "No hyphen. Hunt will be their last name. You know I understand where you're coming from, but I'm not going to let that go. If you really want, their middle name can be Titan. But that's the most I'm going to offer."

"These kids are half mine, Diesel. I don't think it's fair that you demand they carry your last name when I'm the one who created them, who gave birth to them. It's an old sexist practice."

"Even if it is, it's a tradition that's not going to disappear. It'll be confusing for them as they age through life. By having a hyphen, it indicates they have two allegiances—to their mother and father. By having a single last name we all share, it unites us as a family."

She crossed her arms over her chest, but she didn't display that aggressive look she sometimes wore. "Then why don't you change your last name to Titan?"

I wasn't even going to respond to that. I just stared her down, my pissed-off expression doing all the talking.

"It's sexist that I'm expected to take your last name."

"And it would be sexist for a man to take a woman's last name. It goes both ways. No matter what sex gets their way, the other sex will be disappointed. But that's how it works. And there's no way in hell I'm taking your last name, especially in our society. If you thought I was a man who would actually make that sacrifice, you wouldn't be marrying me. We both know it."

She didn't blink or reposition her body in the chair. "Then where does that leave us?"

I admired her strength and aggression, especially in

a world as cold and cruel as ours. That's how she survived and persevered. But in this situation, it really bit me in the ass. "Our children will have my last name. And you need to take my last name too."

"I need to?" she challenged.

"You aren't going to want to have a different last name from your kids. Trust me."

"I suppose I could do Titan-Hunt."

I shook my head. "Baby…"

"You have no idea how difficult this is," she whispered. "My whole life I've been Titan. Now that I've fallen in love, I have to walk away from all of that?"

"But you're inheriting a very powerful last name. It's not a step down."

"It's not about that, Diesel."

"We're combining our lives together. We're becoming one person. I want to hear people call you Mrs. Hunt. I want to hear those words every single day. I want us to be the Hunt family. But that doesn't ruin your legacy."

"It ends it. I'm the last one who carries the name."

"Family lines die out all the time," I said gently. "But the legacy doesn't change. Your father will always be proud of you because of your accomplishments, not because of the credibility you bring to his last name."

She looked away the instant her father was mentioned.

"Titan can be their middle name," I said. "The name won't be lost."

"No one cares about middle names."

"Not true," I countered. "The legacy still carries on. You can change your middle name to Titan too."

"I'm not doing that."

We'd reached a stalemate, and it didn't seem like we could move forward. We couldn't even move backward. We were just stuck. "Baby, I want you to take my last name for a reason other than convenience. I want us to be husband and wife. I want us to be joined together in every way possible. I know this is going to last until the day I die, so I'm not worried about doing this for nothing."

"I'm not worried about it either."

"Then just consider it."

She shook her head slightly.

"Consider it with an open mind."

She turned her gaze back to her food and didn't look at me. Her arms were still crossed over her chest, and in this light, she looked phenomenally beautiful. If she actually became Mrs. Hunt, that would be the sexiest thing in the world. It would suit her perfectly. "I'll think about it…"

# CHAPTER FIVE

THORN

I stepped inside the conference room, a room surrounded by glass walls so anyone walking by could see directly inside. Autumn was visible before I even stepped into the room, wearing a burgundy blouse and black heels. I imagined she was wearing a pencil skirt under the desk—because that's what she usually wore. She had the body to pull it off.

Actually, she had the body to rock it.

I stepped inside and smoothed out the front of my tie. A cart was placed off to the side, full of coffee, cream, and snacks. My eyes were on her, sitting on the other side of the table. Now I had to interact with her as a professional. The last time I saw her, I fucked her on the couch then told her I was a jealous man.

Now I was supposed to shake her hand like that never happened?

Autumn rose from the table and came forward to greet me. "Thorn."

I wanted to extend my hand, but that felt strange. I'd shaken her hand before, but that was before I'd fucked her a dozen times. If someone else were in the room, I would have done it. But right then and there, the last thing I wanted to do was shake her hand. "Autumn, how are you?"

She didn't try to shake my hand either. "Good. I'm excited to get started."

"Then let's begin." I purposely moved to the other side of the table so there would be an appropriate amount of distance between us. If I got too close to her, I was afraid of what I might do. I might grab her thigh under the table because I couldn't keep myself under control. People passed the glass doors as they traveled to their offices or the break room. We were like fish in a bowl, visible for everyone to see.

Why did Titan make all of her rooms like this?

"Can I get you some coffee?" I asked.

"No, thanks. I can get it myself if I want it." She opened her folder and organized her notes.

I wanted to smile because she sounded just like Titan. "Of course."

"So, where do you want to start?" She rested her hands together, her fingers interlocking.

"I'd like to know about your projects. That way Titan can determine what her focus will be. You'll have to dumb it down for me because I'm not much of a science guy." Titan might understand it more, but I worked primarily in the food industry.

"I don't need to dumb it down for you, Thorn. People think science is complicated, but it's not. It's actually very simple." She pulled out a few sheets and slid them toward me. "This is what I've been focusing on…"

She spent the next hour discussing her scientific findings along with the technology she was advancing. She gave me a list of industry purposes for every single innovation, which was very helpful. Once she opened up her world to me, I realized I was dealing with an intellect I'd never encountered before. Her genius was unbelievable. It made me wonder why she was wasting her time on me. I was an idiot compared to her.

"This will be a good advance in the industry," she said. "These changes are cost-effective and affordable for any company, big or small. And in the end, it'll save them a lot of money. I'm not sure how Titan wants to begin marketing this or what angle she's going to choose, but I'm interested in finding out."

I flipped through the pages again and added a few things to my notes. When I was absorbed in the world we were working in, I forgot about the obvious chemistry between us. Work seemed to be the only thing strong enough to distract me for a significant amount of time. But once the meeting was over, like any other man, I would return to thinking about one thing—sex. "Thank you, Autumn. That was very informative."

"I told you I didn't need to dumb it down."

"I won't pretend to understand the science behind it. I'll just have to take your word for it."

"I can always show you my lab, if you're curious."

"I wouldn't mind, actually." She had a few things in her office, but I wouldn't mind seeing where she did the heavy lifting. I imagined it was the size of a warehouse, and all of her work was neatly organized despite the cacophony of information she was processing.

"Just tell me when and where." She closed her folder then eyed her watch. "Is there anything else we should discuss today?"

"I think we've got it covered. I'll go over this with Titan, and we'll go from there."

"When will she be back?" she asked.

"Honestly, I don't know. And I can't ask. If I do—"

"It'll make her anxious to get back to work," she said. "I understand."

A tapping noise sounded on the door before it opened. Diesel walked in, wearing a dark gray suit with a black tie. He showed a charismatic smile as he leaned in the doorway. "Can I come in? Or am I interrupting something?"

"Would it matter?" I asked like a smartass.

He stepped inside and turned to me. "How's it going?"

"Good." I rose to my feet and shook his hand. "Ms. Alexander and I just finished our meeting." I didn't go out of my way to greet anyone with the same respect that I did with Diesel because we had a unique situation. Diesel had been telling the truth, but I hadn't listened to him. He never turned his back on Titan or me despite our negative opinion of him, and that earned a lifetime of respect. I'd always get out of my chair and greet him. He was a good man. "How are you?"

"I'm taking Titan to the doctor this afternoon," he said. "Stitches should be coming out."

"That's great news."

"Things are kinda tense between us right now." He rubbed the back of his neck as his expression hardened.

"Why?" Did he tell Titan about her mom?

"We talked about starting a family, and that led to the dreaded conversation of changing her last name. She's being very stubborn about it."

I held back my chuckle but couldn't stop myself from smiling. "Were you expecting something else?"

"I guess I thought it would be a little easier."

"It won't," I said. "But keep pushing her, and she'll do it. Trust me, she will."

"You think?" he asked.

"Definitely. She loves you. I know she wants to be a Hunt. The only thing holding her back is her father. It's a touchy subject with her."

"Yeah, you're right."

"She'll cave," I said with confidence. "I know she will."

"You do know her better than anyone," he said with a chuckle.

I was her best friend, but I would never know her in the way Diesel did. Deep love like that was something I'd never experienced. Titan was important to me and I would do anything for her, but she wasn't my whole world. "Not anymore." I patted him on the back before I turned to Autumn. "Have you two met before?"

"I don't think so." Autumn came around the desk and shook Diesel's hand. "It's nice to meet you."

"You too." Diesel dropped his hand and placed it in his pocket. "Thorn and Titan have told me a lot of great things about you."

"That's good to know." She held her hands together in front of her waist then turned her gaze on me. She wore a smile, but that joy didn't reach her eyes. There was something else in the look that I couldn't identify.

Diesel turned back to me. "I'll let you guys get back to work. But next time you see Titan…give her a nudge for me. She listens to you."

He gave me way too much credit. "She listens to you more than you realize."

He patted me on the shoulder and headed to the door.

"Let me know how the doctor visit goes."

"Sure thing." Diesel nodded to both of us before he walked out. He stepped through the glass doors then walked down the hallway, looking like he owned the building before he even tied the knot with Titan.

I turned back to Autumn. "I'm sure Diesel will be involved with a lot of things around here after they get married."

"Yeah…" She continued to look at me with hesitance. The calm and confident woman that was there just a moment ago was long gone.

"Everything alright?" I'd been sleeping with her for weeks, and in that time frame, I'd gotten to know her well. I understood her body cues, her moods. I didn't have it down to an exact science just yet, but I would get there.

"I'm fine."

"You seem really tense all of a sudden."

"I guess…never mind." She returned to her seat and sat down.

"Never mind what?" I sank into my chair, my eyes homing in on her face.

"I guess I'm surprised the two of you are so close."

"Who?" I asked me. "Me and Diesel?"

"Yeah."

"Why wouldn't we be?" He was a great guy who was loyal and honest. I'd always seen Titan as a friend, but now that she was marrying him, it was like I getting another friend too. He would be part of our small family.

"Uh…because he's engaged to your ex-fiancée."

I kept forgetting that stupid lie was real to some people. "Yeah, but that was a long time ago."

"It was less than six weeks ago…"

Shit, that was it? It felt like a lifetime had already passed. I couldn't believe I'd only proposed to her a few months ago. The enormous engagement ring was still sitting in my nightstand because I didn't know what to do with it. I could pawn it, but that somehow felt cheap. But I couldn't keep it either. It's not like it had any purpose. "Seems longer than that." I wanted to change the subject because this was dangerous territory. The world was beginning to get used to Titan and Diesel being together, and they weren't focusing on me as much. Maybe Autumn needed more time to forget about the whole thing.

"I'm just surprised you're so close with him considering what happened. I don't think anyone else would be able to handle the situation with such maturity. I mean, you loved this woman and wanted to spend your whole life with her…and then she left you for someone else. I know I wouldn't be able to put on a straight face and shake hands with the woman who took my man away."

I wouldn't either, but I couldn't tell her that. I was tempted to tell her the truth, but since the incident was still so fresh, I knew I had to wait a while. If she told anyone the entire relationship was bogus, it would ruin Titan's reputation. Right now, people were focused on the brave way she fought off her attacker. She was considered to be a hero. I wouldn't take that away from her. "I can spend my time being angry about it, or I can just let it go. I choose to let it go." I turned back to my notes and wrote a few things down.

I knew she was staring at me across the table, those large green eyes glued to my face. Her dark hair was pushed back behind her shoulders, putting her pretty face right in the forefront.

I looked up to see her straight-on look. "What?"

She finally broke eye contact. "Nothing."

———

The game was on the TV, and I sat in the living room with a bottle of beer resting on a coaster. It'd been a long day at the office, tons of paperwork and meetings. The only highlight of the day was seeing Autumn.

Damn, those eyes.

I loved the way they sparkled, like jewels. She was prettier than a doll and sexier than a model. She had everything the ideal woman should possess—brain and sass. I liked everything about her, not just the beauty between her legs.

That was why I was thinking about her now.

I missed her.

I grabbed my phone and sent a text. *Thinking about you.*

*Yeah?*

*Yeah.*

*What exactly are you thinking about that includes me?*

*You naked on my bed.*

*Interesting. Now I'm thinking the same thing.*

I grinned at her banter, loving the way she was naturally playful. *Come over. I'll make dinner.* It was earlier than when we usually saw each other.

*You know how to cook?*

*Not a Thanksgiving feast, but I can make a few things. What do you say?*

*Hmm...free food and good sex.*

I grinned wider. *That sounds like a pretty good deal to me. I'll be over in a bit.*

*Looking forward to it.* I hopped off the couch the second the conversation was over and got to work in the kitchen. I didn't want to do anything too basic because I wanted to impress her, so I made chicken Marsala on a bed of noodles along with mushrooms and broccoli. The second I was finished and the pans were soaking in the sink, the elevator beeped with her arrival.

I was there when the doors opened, standing in just my sweatpants. Anytime I was home, I was shirtless. Sitting in my own skin was the most comfortable position, so I enjoyed it when I wasn't in the office. I was used to wearing a stiff suit all day, a thick tie wrapped around my neck.

She was in jeans and a tight black sweater, dressed casually but sexy at the same time. She could have come in just a towel, and I would have grinned just the way I was now. Dark red lipstick was on her mouth, and her eyelashes were thick and seductive. I'd never seen her without makeup, but I imagined she would look just as beautiful without it. I whistled under my breath and looked her up and down. "I like a woman in jeans."

"Well, you're going to like me, then." She stepped into my penthouse then moved right in for a kiss. Her hand wrapped around my neck, and she stood on her tiptoes to kiss me. The passion in her lips told me she'd wanted to kiss me for the last half hour, that she'd been thinking about me since I texted her.

I grabbed her and pulled her tightly against my body, feeling her perfect curves right against my hard chest. My fingers dug into her jeans then migrated to her ass. My hands dug in and gripped both cheeks.

I loved that ass.

She was the first one to introduce tongue, and she gave it to me with vigor. She pulled me deeper into her, like she hadn't seen me in weeks rather than a few hours. After the tense way we ended things at the office, this was a complete flip.

"You really have been thinking about me..." I smiled against her mouth, feeling my self-worth double just like it was a holding in the stock market.

Her hand pressed against my hard-on in my sweat-pants. "Just as you've been thinking about me..." She batted her eyelashes playfully then walked away from me, her hand sliding across my crotch until she passed me.

Dumbfounded, I stood there for a moment. Her confidence was sexy. I hadn't met a woman who held

so much power and wasn't afraid to show her aware-
ness of it. She didn't pretend to be humble about
her gifts.

When I could finally stop thinking about her hand
against my crotch, I turned around and escorted her
into the dining room. "Hungry?"

"Definitely."

I pulled out the chair for her before I took the seat
across from her. "Wine?"

She sat down and pushed her glass across the hardwood table. "Please."

I filled both of our glass before I placed a napkin in
my lap.

She picked up her silverware and stared at me
instead of cutting into her food.

"You can't stare at me all night. Come on, eat."

"Do you always eat with your shirt off?"

"Whenever I'm home."

"That looks dangerous…"

"How?"

"You spill a hot piece of chicken on your chest…
and that will definitely burn."

"Well, I don't spill." I cut into my food and took
a bite.

"Alright…" She finally directed her gaze to her
dinner and placed a bite in her mouth. "Wow…this
is good."

"Don't be surprised."

She continued to eat, enjoying everything on her

plate and washing it down with some wine. "Who taught you how to cook?"

"My mom."

She was about to drink from her wine again but stopped herself. She suppressed the smile on her mouth, but it couldn't be contained behind those gorgeous, plump lips. "Your mom?"

"Yeah? So what."

"I've never heard a man say that before."

"My mom was a stay-at-home mom most of her life. Whenever I'd come home from school, I'd ask her for a snack. She always told me she wouldn't make it for me, but she would always make it *with* me. I guess that was her way of making me more independent. She started doing it when I was five, which is a little young, but it paid off."

"That's cute."

"Yeah, I've always been a bit of a mama's boy. Make fun of me all you want. I don't give a damn." I'd also lived in a house with my brother and father, so it was all sports and activities. My younger brother needed more attention than I did, so my dad gave it to him. That left me to hang out with Mom.

"Why would I make fun of you?"

"Because no grown-ass man should say he's a mama's boy."

"I don't see the harm. I'm a daddy's girl."

"Not the same thing. That's actually cute."

"You're cute too, Thorn."

I drank my wine again, brushing off her comment. "You're just saying that because you're in love with my big dick."

She chuckled. "I'm not saying that because I'm in love with your dick. I'm saying it because it's true."

"Whatever you say…"

"If I were just in love with your package, I wouldn't be having dinner with you. I'd get my action and then take off." She'd already eaten half of her food, and she was still going. "Keep that in mind."

"That's a good point. I don't have dinner with women either."

"Never?" she asked incredulously.

I shook my head. "I don't think I've ever cooked for a woman before."

"Not even Titan?" she asked in surprise.

"Well, except for her. But that's a different situation."

"Because she's the only woman you've ever loved?"

"Uh…" I didn't like the way she phrased that. It made me sound like a pussy. "No. Because we would work late at my place, and I would just whip something up. It wasn't really romantic…"

She swirled her wine before she took a drink, her mood suddenly diving. "I know it's hard right now, but it'll get easier."

Huh? What was she talking about? "What will get easier?"

"Getting over her." She started to push her food

around, obviously no longer hungry. Her eyes turned down to her food for a while before she raised them again.

My immediate response was to laugh at the absurdity of her words. I couldn't get over Titan because I never felt a romantic feeling toward her. I wanted to blurt that out and tell her I'd never loved a woman in all my life. Just when I decided to, she kept talking.

"I've been through something similar. It's one of those things that takes time. It's different for everyone. Some people immediately bounce back, and some people don't." Her eyes were filled with painful memories, and her somberness escaped in her tone. The indications were subtle, but since I paid such attention to her, the signs were obvious to me.

Now I didn't care about setting the record straight. All I cared about was what caused her to feel so much anguish. How could a man leave her for someone else when she was absolutely perfect? The guy would have to be insane. "You have?"

"Yeah." She set her utensils down, obviously finished eating. "It's been a few years now. But for the first six months, I was pretty upset about it. As time passed, it got easier. I'm in a good place now, and I'm very happy. But I'm so happy that I'm scared to lose it again. So that makes it impossible to trust anyone. I'm not sure if I'll ever want to be in a relationship again. Not when it seems so risky."

My heart tightened in pain, and I ached for this

woman. I never wanted her to be sad. I never wanted her to be so hurt that she couldn't trust again. Whoever this guy was, I knew he would regret his decision someday—big-time. "What happened?"

"The specifics don't matter. I was in love with this guy, and we were happy together. He started a new job, met someone there, and unfortunately, it just happened. It wasn't a situation where he was sneaking around behind my back and lying about where he was. He told me he was attracted to her. A month later, he left his job because he couldn't be around her anymore. But that was when he realized that whatever they had was some-thing he couldn't ignore. So he left…" She said all of it with surprising strength, but there was a hint of the years of pain that she endured. "Months went by, and I constantly questioned if I was the problem. If I'd done my hair differently or worked out more, would he have stayed? But in the end, I knew it was out of my control. Perhaps this woman was his soul mate, and there was nothing either of us could have done about it. I saw him about eight months ago. They're married and have a young daughter together. It took me a long time to look him in the eye and say I was happy for him…but I am happy for him."

She was a lot more understanding than I was. I wanted to crush this guy's skull with my bare hands. How could he possibly think this other woman was better than Autumn? How could he walk away from such a remarkable woman? "I'm sorry, Autumn."

"Don't be. It took me a long time to understand that being young is about finding the right person. I obviously wasn't the right person for him, and he followed his instincts. He was always honest with me, so how could I hate him? I know the whole thing caused him pain too."

Not enough pain, if you asked me.

"But now that I'm happy on my own, I don't want to go down that road again. Being by myself feels a lot safer. I'm very protective of my happiness, and I'm not sure if I could risk it for someone again…"

Her perspective made complete sense to me. She'd loved a man, but that love wasn't good enough for him. That kind of rejection stung forever. But I didn't want to feel that way, to feel scared of loving someone. "You shouldn't give up. He wasn't the man you're supposed to be with, because the real guy is still out there somewhere."

"Maybe…maybe not." Her eyes drifted away, leaving the conversation as her thoughts swirled behind her eyes.

I abandoned my food because I lost my appetite. Her pain shocked my whole system so I wasn't interested in my dinner, no matter how good it was. Now I wanted to make her feel better, to do anything to pull her from this misery. "He made the biggest mistake of his life, Autumn."

"I've seen them together, and I don't think he did." A soft smile formed on her lips. "I guess that's why I'm okay with it. I wouldn't go out of my way to be nice to the woman he married the way you are with Diesel… but I don't hate her."

Now I felt like a jerk for lying to her. She only told me that story because she thought I was going through the same thing. I wanted to correct her, but I thought that might embarrass her. I didn't know what to do, so I didn't do anything. "Thanks for telling me…"

"I see the way you are with Titan, and I know you're going through it too. But it must be hard to see the love of your life on a regular basis…"

I hid my cringe as best as I could. "It's…it's not as intense as you think it is."

"And I understand why you don't want a relationship either. I can't blame you. Having good sex with someone with no expectations is a lot easier. You don't get your hopes up, you don't get your trust up, and you know the arrangement has a deadline. It takes all the emotional bullshit out of it."

I wanted the same thing, but for different reasons. I was incapable of love, so I just wanted lust. I'd never had my heart broken because I couldn't fall in love in the first place. If I told her that, she would think I was crazy—as she should. "Do you want to have a family?"

"I do…eventually. I'm not sure how right now, but I've always wanted kids."

That was something I wanted too, to have my own family. I needed a wife for that, but without love, I would never find anyone, unless it was a mail-order bride. Titan was different because she had the same desires I did.

But then I realized Autumn did too.

She wanted the exact same thing…

Autumn turned back to me, and her eyes narrowed as she looked into mine. "What?"

I knew she was commenting on the new expression I wore, the brightness in my eyes at my discovery. I didn't know what to do with this information because I'd just uncovered it, but I definitely wanted to put it to use—just not right now. "Nothing."

# CHAPTER SIX

VINCENT

I arrived at the restaurant first and sat there alone. A single candle flickered in the center of the table, and a bottle of my favorite wine was there. My glass had been poured, but I didn't drink from it because it felt rude to start without her.

I never offered to pick up Scarlet because that felt too intimate.

Like it was a date.

I wasn't sure what this was. Up until that point, I hadn't been really thinking about my actions that much. I was just doing things...doing things that I wanted to do. I knew I enjoyed Scarlet's company so I kept requesting more of her time even though I had no idea where it would go.

I wasn't sure if I wanted it to go anywhere.

It was easy for me to bed women like Alessia

because I knew it was meaningless. It wasn't like I loved any of the women who came after Isabella. They were warm bodies in my sheets, beautiful women to satisfy my physical needs. I was a sexual man, even at my age in life. But I didn't feel ashamed for those necessities.

No one judged me for that.

But to actually care about someone…that was different.

I hadn't done more than shake Scarlet's hand, but I felt like I'd already touched her everywhere.

It felt wrong.

It felt right.

I didn't notice her approach because I was too busy wrestling with my own guilt. I wanted to justify what I was doing, but there was no excuse to mask what was really happening.

I liked Scarlet.

I rose to my feet just as she reached the table. She was in a sweetheart-top black dress that was tight around her waist. It stopped just above her knee, and her black pumps gave her a few extra inches. Her hair was pulled back, revealing the beautiful skin of her neck and chest. She looked beautiful in a classic way, but she also looked stunning in other ways…

In ways that made me wonder how that olive skin would look against my sheets.

I'd been attracted to other women before, even strongly.

But my attraction to Scarlet was much more intense —in a lot of ways. "You look lovely."

"Thank you." She wore earrings dangling from her lobes, and they caught the light every time she shifted slightly. "You look nice too."

I pulled out the chair for her then moved to the other side of the table. I didn't even touch her waist or greet her with a hug. I avoided touching her at all costs, like she was fire and my fingers might get burned.

"Wine?" I held up the bottle.

"Please."

I poured her a glass then set the bottle on the other side of the table. There was already a basket of bread, but I hadn't touched anything because it would have been rude. But then again, I didn't eat bread so it wouldn't have mattered.

She placed her clutch at the edge of the table then picked up the menu. "I haven't been here before, but I hear good things."

"I've had a few meetings here. The food is great, and the service is quick."

Her eyes browsed the selections. "Any recommendations?"

"The duck is exquisite. But the tenderloin is also good. If you're looking for something on the healthier side, they have a great vegan option. I've had that for lunch a few times."

She smiled as she kept looking. "Well, I'm not looking for anything healthy. When I go out to dinner, I make the most out of it." She chuckled and didn't lift up her gaze.

I was glad she didn't because I got to enjoy the view of her. She'd just had her nails done, a classy French tip look. Her eye makeup was different, but I couldn't explain how. I loved the way she enjoyed herself rather than starved herself. Alessia always got a salad and an ice water. She didn't even drink wine most of the time because of the sugar and calories.

Made our dates a little boring.

"Then what are you getting?"

"Carbs."

I almost chuckled.

"I'm getting the pasta." She finally shut the menu. "What about you?"

"I don't want to say."

"Why not?" She wrapped her fingers around the stem of the wine glass.

"I guess I don't make the most out of dinners like you do."

Her smile hadn't faded away. "Please don't tell me you're getting a salad."

I shrugged in guilt.

"Come on, live a little." She took a drink, her lipstick immediately sticking to the glass.

"I've noticed it's harder to keep my appearance up as I've aged."

"I know that all too well," she said. "Especially after

I had my daughter. But sometimes, you just have to stop caring."

I'd always been fit since I was in my twenties. Physical exercise and diet had become an essential part of my routine. Since I didn't have a wife to cook for me, it was easy to stick to a clean diet. I wouldn't land women like Alessia if I didn't keep a strong figure. "It's hard for me not to care."

"Because you're one of the sexiest bachelors in the city? Or the country, for that matter?"

I didn't view myself in that light, but I was flattered she did. "You think that?"

She laughed like my question was absurd. "You're a very good-looking man, Vincent. You brush your teeth in the mirror every day…you must know this."

I was aware of my charms, but I was happy she was aware of them too. "I'm flattered."

"You shouldn't be. It's the truth."

The waiter arrived and took our order.

I let Scarlet go first.

"I'll take the pasta—extra cheese." She handed the menu over.

The corner of my mouth rose in a smile.

"And you, Mr. Hunt?" the waiter asked, recognizing me like most other people.

Scarlet sipped her wine as she watched me.

I handed the menu over. "Give me the same thing—just not the extra cheese."

"Very good, sir." He walked away.

Scarlet was grinning from ear to ear. "Now, that's more like it."

————

When we finished dinner, we left the restaurant and reached the sidewalk. My driver immediately pulled up in my car and parked at the curb, aware of my movements at all times. I texted him two minutes ahead of time, and he was always at the right spot by the time I needed him.

"Thank you for dinner." Scarlet held her clutch in her hand and walked slowly beside me, her heels clapping against the concrete. "I hope you don't regret skipping the salad."

"Not even a little bit." It was okay to cheat once in a while.

"Good. I definitely don't regret it." She rubbed her flat stomach and stopped in front of my car.

"Can I give you a ride home?"

"Yes, thank you." I opened the back door for her and helped her inside. Then I sat beside her and closed the divider between the driver and us. Scarlet gave him the address over the speaker, and then we were moving through the streets.

I hadn't put up the divider because I planned on doing anything inappropriate. I just wanted some privacy. I wanted to be able to talk to her without someone listening in. Ironically, we didn't say anything on the trip to her apartment. I'd dropped her off before but had never been inside the building. She lived in a good part of town. It wasn't anything like where Diesel and I lived, but it was definitely nice.

My driver pulled up to the curb, and I got out first. I gave her my hand so she could use it for balance as she slid her beautiful legs out of the car. She stepped on the sidewalk then held herself perfectly straight.

I shut the back door and walked her to the front door of her building. "I had a great time tonight."

"Me too."

I opened the door and held it open so she could walk inside.

But she didn't cross the threshold. "I always have a nice time with you, Vincent. You're very easy to talk to."

"Thanks. I think the same about you."

Her eyes shifted back and forth slightly as she looked at me, the green color of her eyes reflecting the fluorescent lights from inside the building. A few strands of her hair came loose, floating in the slight breeze that billowed through the city. As the silence passed, it didn't seem like she was going to walk inside. It seemed like she wanted to stay out there with me...in the cold.

Then she leaned into me, rising on the tips of her toes, and pressed a kiss to the corner of my mouth.

I closed my eyes when I felt her warm lips, felt the softness I'd been thinking about for a week. My hand stayed on the door, and I kissed her back, my movements just as slow as hers. She kissed me like she didn't know what would happen once she touched me. I kissed her with the same hesitance, like I crossed an invisible line I'd never crossed before.

She pulled away, her eyes lidded with the spark that erupted between our mouths. "Would you like to come up?"

The question stunned me even when it shouldn't. I'd been going out of my way to see her for weeks now without actually asking her on a date. I called her assistant just to figure out how she preferred her coffee. I willingly told her things I wouldn't have told another reporter. It was obvious how I felt about this woman— and now it was obvious to her.

I didn't know if this invitation was just for coffee after dinner, but I suspected that wasn't the case. As enticing as it was to finish that kiss we just had, some-thing held me back. It was fear, guilt, and a lot of other things. "I would love to…but I don't think I'm ready for that."

"Oh…" She couldn't mask her disappointment. The embarrassment formed in her eyes, the rejection stinging her.

I didn't want to make her feel bad, but I couldn't go up there. There was too much guilt in my chest, too much pain. "Good night, Scarlet." I leaned and kissed her on the cheek. Then I turned away and headed back to the car without looking back.

I got into the back seat and told my driver to immediately pull away. That way I wouldn't have to see if she was still standing there. The darkness of the back seat surrounded me, and the classical music overhead blocked out some of my thoughts—but not all.

All I could think about was the empty penthouse I was about to return to.

I didn't want to be there.

I wanted to be in Scarlet's apartment.

But the guilt kept me away.

———

Tatum moved into my arms and gave me a strong squeeze.

I hugged her back, immediately smiling at the affection she just gave me. It was the best I'd ever seen her, the most I'd seen her move. She hugged me hard like there wasn't anything restraining her anymore.

"You look great," I said into her hair.

"I feel great." She pulled away then rubbed her hand across the left side of her chest. "My stitches were finally removed."

"That's great, Tatum. I'm very happy to hear that."

Like a pregnant woman, she had a wonderful glow to her. Her happiness was rising as her health returned. She'd made an extraordinary recovery, and the worst had passed. "Does that mean you'll be joining us at work? Kyle and I have made a lot of progress together. Products are already on their way to distribution."

"No." Diesel interfered, like always. "She's not going back just yet, but soon." He was in dark jeans and a t-shirt, obviously taking the day off to be with her.

Tatum didn't hide her annoyed expression just because I was there. "Hopefully, very soon…"

"You have to do it right, baby," Diesel said. "You've come this far. Don't take a shortcut now."

She rolled her eyes and walked away. "You've made your point very clear."

Diesel turned back to me. "She's feeling better, but she's more restless."

"Would you like something to drink?" Tatum called from the kitchen.

"No, I'm okay," I answered. "But thank you."

Diesel walked me to the couch. "How's it going, Dad?"

"Good. I'm glad to see things are going well with you."

"They're alright." He sat on the other couch. "Tatum and I are having some arguments about the wedding."

Every couple had their preferences, and there was bound to be clashing. Isabella and I went through the same. "You want my advice, son?"

"I didn't ask for it."

"Well, I'm going to give it to you anyway, smartass," I snapped. "Just give her whatever she wants."

Diesel released a fake chuckle and shook his head. "Normally, I would. But not this time."

Tatum joined us and set a glass of water in front of me even though I'd rejected her offer. She sat beside Diesel and crossed her legs.

Diesel kept his gaze on me. "But maybe you can give her some advice. Titan doesn't want to take my last name when we get married."

Any disagreements about their marriage shouldn't involve me, but I did chime in once. "A lot of women don't change their name nowadays."

"Yes, but when they have children, it makes things complicated," Diesel said. "And Titan wants our children to have her last name or have a hyphen, which just isn't going to work. We've talked about it a few times, but she won't budge."

I understood a woman like Titan prided herself on her independence, and since people referred to her as Titan all the time, she would be completely changing her identity. She was a person who needed control in her life. Changing her name would put her under someone else's control, in a way. "Diesel, you know this isn't any of my business."

Diesel sighed in disappointment.

"Thank you, Vincent," Tatum said. "Diesel hasn't been very understanding about the matter."

"With all due respect," he said to her. "My kids will have my last name. I'm not letting you call them Titan-Hunt."

I didn't want my grandkids to have a different last name from me either, but I still held my silence. I shouldn't even be listening to this conversation. "Your mom and I didn't agree on everything. I found the secret to a happy marriage is compromise. Meet half-way. Or have one person compromise on this and the other person compromise on something else later."

"Kinda hard to compromise on this," Diesel said quietly.

"I'm sure the two of you will figure it out." I wanted to stay, but judging by the tension between them, I should leave. "I should get going. I've got a few things to take care of at the office."

Tatum walked me to the door, leaving her sour look behind on the couch with Diesel. "I'm sorry Diesel put you in an awkward position. He's just angry with me right now." She reached the elevator then hit the button.

"I understand," I said. "Just keep in mind why he feels that way."

She hugged me then pulled away. "What do you mean?"

"When a man takes a wife, she belongs to him. It's a possessive type of thing. He wants to take care of you for the rest of your life, so he wants you to wear his last name...so everyone will know you're his." The doors opened, and I stepped inside. "I felt the exact same way when I got married. Consider it romantic."

———

Five days passed, and I didn't reach out to Scarlet.

She didn't contact me either.

The last night I saw her didn't end well. I knew rejecting her offer hurt her. She made the first move and kissed me, then she took it a step further. The problem wasn't the kiss…I enjoyed the kiss.

But I wished she'd let me make the move when I was ready.

Even though I didn't know if I would ever be ready.

I wasn't avoiding her. I knew I had to talk to her eventually because of the article she wrote. That conversation could go in either direction. She might be cold and distant to me, unable to forgive the way I hurt her. Or she might pretend it never happened and let the tension grow between us.

I didn't know what to expect.

I was sitting in my office when my assistant spoke through the intercom. "I have Scarlet Blackwood here to see you."

I knew I didn't have an appointment with her, and I didn't need to double-check. "Send her in."

A moment later, Scarlet walked inside my office. She was in a black pencil skirt with a white blouse, looking thin and beautiful. She held two large manila envelopes in her hand, and her usual smile was absent. Her happiness didn't fill the room like it usually did. She wasn't intimidated by me, but she also didn't seem thrilled to be there. "Hello, Vincent." Clipped and cold, her tone suggested this conversation was entirely business.

I rose to my feet. "Hey, Scarlet."

She stopped in front of my desk and held up the two folders. "I wanted to drop these off."

One must be the photographs, and the other must be the article. "That was kind of you."

She set them on the surface of my desk and pressed her finger against once. "This is the article I'm going to publish. I did as you asked and excluded all topics you didn't want to discuss. I'm going to publish as it is in forty-eight hours unless you tell me otherwise." She pushed the other envelope toward me. "This isn't the version I'm publishing…but this is the version I wanted to write. This is what I really think…how I really feel." She held my gaze for several heartbeats before she pulled her hand away. "If I don't hear from you…take care." She turned around and left my office, gliding across the floor with the elegance of a queen.

I had a meeting in fifteen minutes, but that no longer seemed important. All I cared about was the envelope sitting on my desk, the article she penned with such honesty. I wanted to know what it said, and I wanted to discover why she wrote it in the first place.

I sat down and pulled it out. Then I began to read.

## Vincent Hunt: They Don't Make Men Like This Anymore.

*By: Scarlet Blackwood, Editor In Chief*

*When Vincent Hunt agreed to do an article with Platform, I only cared about how much our readers would love to know more about this enigma. Quiet and mysterious, Vincent Hunt is a man who stays out of the spotlight as much as possible. Unfortunately, that makes him more interesting—the last thing he wants. Within our first conversation, I realized I'd been mining for gold but uncovered royal treasure instead.*

*Vincent Hunt is an extraordinary man.*

*Despite his billions, he never mentioned his wealth once. His romantic connections with the biggest supermodels of the world weren't mentioned either. A man of very few words, he said more with his coffee-colored eyes than that chiseled jaw of his. In his mid-fifties, he makes men in their twenties look out of shape. Full of gentle kindness and chivalric masculinity, Vincent Hunt is a man far above the rest.*

*He told me about his complicated relationship with his family, and instead of seeing a defensive and proud man argue his opinion, I saw a father profess his love for all three of his sons. It didn't matter what was said between them. At the end of it all, Vincent Hunt loves his family more than anything on this earth. Strip away his expensive suit, fancy watch, and the billions sitting in his wallet, he's just like the rest of us. He's a parent.*

*I felt my knees growing weaker by the second.*

*The instant Vincent Hunt pulled on the new line of suits, it seemed like they were made just for him. The fabric molded to his musculature, and his expansive chest stretched his collared shirt in just the right way. He never smiled for any of the photographs, but that intense expensive he wore made the suits look better anyway.*

*What I love most is fashion. I care about the feel of every fabric, the way it smells once it's delivered. But being with Vincent Hunt made me forget the suits and focus on the man underneath the material.*

*It started off with a lunch meeting, but then we bumped into each other at a fashion show. Then it led to lunch, a tour of a famous museum, and then a beautiful candlelight dinner. I told myself not to let my heart run off with Vincent Hunt, but every time I looked into those brown eyes, I got lost.*

*He was too good to be true. He was a man every woman wanted. Kind, honest, rugged, and a pure gentleman. He'd aged like a fine wine, and I'd never seen a man more handsome than the one who barely touched me.*

*But I knew Vincent Hunt was complicated for a reason.*

*A widower of more than a decade, he still carried a vigil for his wife in his heart. She was a ghost every new woman would have to compete with, and of course, she would always win.*

*His love for his wife never bothered me. I respected it, understood it.*

*But I wondered if he had room for one more person, even if it was just a small amount of space in his heart.*

*I'm beginning to see that Vincent Hunt prefers physical relationships because they don't make him feel anything. There's no reason to feel guilty when there's nothing to feel guilty about.*

*But that's not what I want.*

*I want those conversations, those walks through the museum. I want to know the man underneath the suit, to have more than just a relationship—but a friendship. No man in my entire life has made my heart beat so fast, has made me feel like I'm not too old to fall in love.*

*So I'm going to tell him how I feel and hope for the best.*

*I'm not asking for forever.*

*All I'm asking is for a chance.*

*Because Vincent Hunt is a man I'm willing to be patient with. And he's the only man I'm willing to share with another woman. He's worth the risk, worth this confession.*

*He's worth it all.*

I finished the last page and set it on my desk. The black letters contrasted against the cream paper and stood out to me in bold. I wanted to read it again, but I knew it would say the same thing.

Scarlet understood me better than I realized.

Perhaps I wasn't as clever as I thought.

My hands came together in my lap, and my fingers touched. I considered the article again, going through the different points she made. It was unbelievably flattering and so honest that my respect for her continued to grow.

I blew her off on her doorstep, but she still made another move.

And it was a good move.

The idea of calling her was tempting. I wanted to invite her to my place for an intimate dinner. I wanted to learn more about her daughter, about the things in life that made her happy. I also wanted those quiet moments when we didn't say anything at all. That peaceful silence was what I valued most in a relationship. I wasn't a strong conversationalist. All I could do was be direct about what I wanted. But talking for pleasure…wasn't my strength.

And I wanted to do other things with her.

I wanted to make love to her.

The second I let the thought enter my mind, I felt the burn of betrayal. I felt unfaithful to Isabella. She was the only woman I'd ever made love to. Alessia, Meredith, and all the others were nothing but good fucks. The distinction was clear, and I never crossed it.

I'd waited long enough to move on, but now that the moment was there, I wasn't sure if I could do it.

I couldn't.

———

It would be cheap to do this over the phone, so I waited outside her office building until she left work.

She stepped out in the same outfit she'd been wearing when she stopped by my office.

I emerged from the side of the building and walked up to her. She didn't realize I was there, so I said her name. "Scarlet."

She stopped at the sound of my voice and turned to me, her eyes unable to hide their surprise. She didn't have any warning, so she needed a few seconds to compose herself. "Hello, Vincent. I didn't see you there…"

"It's alright." We stood away from the pedestrians

on the sidewalk. The foot traffic became more saturated as everyone else got off work and headed to the gym or home. Now that I was face-to-face with her, this suddenly became much harder. "I liked the article."

She held her purse over her shoulder, the unease obvious in her gaze. "I'm glad…"

"You should publish it."

"Great." She cleared her throat. "And the other article…?" It was the first time she looked away, glancing at the ground so she could have a break from my intense stare, the one she liked so much.

I didn't want to hurt this woman, not when I'd become so fond of her. But I didn't want to drag her on and hope for more. It was my fault for leading her on in the first place. I shouldn't have asked her to breakfast and dinner so many times. I shouldn't have put her in this position in the first place. "Everything you said about me is true. You know me better than I realized."

She gave a slight nod.

"I like you, Scarlet. We both know that. But…I don't think I can do this."

She closed her eyes briefly, swallowing the painful answer she didn't want to hear.

"Alessia and Meredith…they're just companions. They don't mean anything to me. But you do mean something to me…and that's why it feels wrong. I thought I could move on, but I don't think I can. My wife…she'll always be there."

"I understand, Vincent," she whispered. "But keep in mind I've never asked you to forget about her."

"I know…but I feel like I'm betraying her."

She was quiet, her hands moving into the pockets of her jacket. She glanced at the people on the sidewalk then turned back to me. "I accept your decision, Vincent. And I appreciate your coming down to tell me in person. But as a friend, I feel like I should say this to you."

"I'm listening."

"If I were lucky enough to have married you, I know I would want you to move on. I know I would want another woman to take care of you, to put away your laundry, cook dinner, and make you happy. We only have so much time on this earth…we should make the best of it." She moved into me and rose on her tiptoes before she planted a kiss on my cheek. Then she quickly turned away, avoiding eye contact with me. "Take care, Vincent."

I watched her walk away, feeling the burn of her kiss branded into my skin. The heels of her pumps clapped against the concrete as she walked away. I listened to the tap as it faded away until it was gone altogether. I felt Scarlet walk out of my life forever.

I didn't think it would hurt this much.

But it did.

## CHAPTER SEVEN

TITAN

Thorn stopped by before Diesel got home, and we went over the progress he and Ms. Alexander were making at the office. Now that I saw all of her projects laid out in front of me, I realized making her a partner was the best decision I'd ever made.

She had a lot to offer.

Having possession of these kinds of developments would change the direction of the company. By constantly having new technology to deliver to consumers, there would always be something to look forward to. People would wait on pins and needles in anticipation of what was next. Older products would become cheaper, so more lines of businesses could afford them.

Now that I knew the full extent of Ms. Alexander's

capabilities, I realized I never would have been able to compete with her.

She would have crushed me.

"You made the right call, Thorn."

He sat across from me at the dining table, enjoying a cold bottle of beer while the papers were scattered in front of us. He was in a gray suit with a black tie, a beard coming in around his jaw. "In what way?"

"Ms. Alexander. I consider myself to be a smart and talented woman, but compared to her intellect, I wouldn't have been able to compete with her, not with this kind of technology. My marketing would always be superior to hers, but without a better product, it wouldn't have mattered."

He nodded slightly. "You should trust me more."

"I already trust you with my life. How could I trust you more?"

He smiled before he drank from his beer. "She's an exceptional woman. I think this partnership will be fruitful for a long time. Not to mention, she's easy to get along with. She doesn't have an attitude or a drop of arrogance. She concentrates on the work and nothing else."

I noticed Thorn always had a lot of nice things to say about her, and his compliments were excessive. He didn't speak highly of anyone else, not even Vincent Hunt or Kyle Livingston. "She's off-limits, Thorn. I know she's cute and smart, but there are plenty of other fish in the sea."

A blank look came over his face. "What?"

"She's my business partner now. Do you have any idea how complicated that would be if you fooled around with her?" He'd see her for a while and then take off. Then it would be awkward anytime they were both in the same room together. Thorn was my best friend, and she and I would probably become great friends too. It was a recipe for disaster.

Thorn slowly brought the bottle to his lips and took a drink.

I organized the papers and returned them to the folder. "So, Diesel and I can't come to an agreement about my last name."

Thorn was still drinking, downing the entire contents in a single gulp.

"You need some water?"

He finished the bottle then wiped his mouth with the back of his hand. "I'm good."

"I understand where he's coming from, but it's such a difficult sacrifice for me."

Thorn cleared his throat before he looked at me again. "You've had that last name your entire life, so it's difficult to part with. It makes sense. I mean, I've been calling you Titan for ten years now. Once you get married, what will I call you? Tatum? It'll be strange at first, but it'll happen. So the change will be difficult in the beginning. But maybe you see it as a way to reinvent yourself. You started off as Titan, but now you're taking a step into a more powerful position by becoming a Hunt."

"Why is it more powerful?"

"You're combining all of your assets with Diesel's. That means the two of you will become the richest couple in the world...let that settle in for just a second."

I didn't care about the money because I had plenty of it, but to reach that kind of status was mind-blowing. I knew I wouldn't reach that position on my own, and neither would Diesel. But, together, we made it happen.

"As Titan, you were the richest woman in the world. Now you'll be one of the richest *people* in the world. Big fucking deal."

It was a big deal.

"Titan won't be lost because everyone will remember where you came from. The name isn't as important as you think it is. It's all about the person. And by taking Diesel's last name, you'll truly be unified with the man you love. I'm not a romantic guy, but if I were, my wife would definitely take my last name. There would be no discussion about it."

"Why?"

"Because it's hot. If some woman stole my heart and I couldn't live without her, I'd be making her mine in every way possible. You bet your ass she would be a Cutler. Not only would her big-ass ring tell the world she was taken, but wearing my last name would tell the world who she was taken by. And unless I'm mistaken, you enjoy Diesel's possessiveness, right?"

I could lie and say I didn't, but Thorn would see right through it. "Yes." I liked being Diesel's, and I liked that he was proud I was his. I used to enjoy being in control all the time, but now I loved having a man who wanted to dominate me all the time. He wanted to take care of me, love me, and make me his in whatever way he could.

"Then let him have you."

After talking to Thorn, it didn't feel so difficult.

"To honor the man you love, give him something that you've never given anyone before. Give him you— all of you."

I smiled at the sweet words Thorn said. "I didn't realize you were so romantic, Thorn."

"I'm not," he argued. "But I know how it feels to want to have a woman all to yourself."

"You do?" I questioned. Last time I checked, he never cared about any woman he'd ever been with. They were all flings, all women who didn't mind the control he needed. They just wanted good sex and expensive gifts. Thorn never seemed possessive of anyone, and he'd never told me otherwise.

Thorn ignored the question. "Despite what we thought, Diesel has been loyal to you from the very beginning. He never lied, and he always stood by you. Even when we cast him out, he didn't give up. He's earned it, Titan. He earned you a long time ago."

When Thorn laid everything out like that, it actually made me want to take Diesel's last name. It didn't feel like such a sacrifice anymore. "Did Diesel put you up to this?"

"He asked me to talk to you about it. But all those opinions are my own."

I knew Thorn wouldn't lie to me. "Then what will you call me?"

He considered it, grinding his teeth together slightly and moving his jaw. "Hunt."

"Yeah?"

"I think it fits."

"Yeah…it does fit."

The elevator beeped just before the doors opened. Diesel stepped inside with his tie already undone. He stripped off his jacket and hung it up on the coatrack. "Hey."

"What's up?" Thorn asked from his seat. "Your woman and I were just talking about work."

"She's not supposed to talk about work," Diesel said ominously. "But I've given up telling her not to."

"Which is smart," I said. "Because you've been wasting your time for a while."

Diesel turned that smoldering gaze on me, making me the sole recipient of that heated look. He approached me at the table then leaned down to kiss me on the lips. The only reason the embrace was quick was because Thorn was sitting right there. "How are you feeling?"

"Great." The stitches were gone, and now only a scar remained behind. I was almost finished with my medications, and the spasms of pain and fatigue had decreased considerably. I was counting down the days until I was well enough to go to work—and get married. "How was your day?"

"The same as all the others." He drifted into the kitchen and fetched a bottle of beer. He twisted off the cap with his big hands and tossed the cap on the table. "How are things coming along for the two of you?"

"Good," Thorn answered. "Working with Ms. Alexander was a smart move."

"She's exceptionally bright," I said. "I've never met anyone with her kind of intellect."

Diesel took a drink as he stared at me. "I have." He turned to the living room and took a seat on the couch.

Thorn must have picked up on the sexual tension in the room because he made his exit. "I should get going. I'll talk to you tomorrow, Titan."

I walked him to the elevator and watched him disappear behind the doors. Then I approached Diesel on the couch, who immediately stood up when I came near. He pulled his tie out of his collar then unbuttoned his shirt, his eyes locked on mine.

"There's something I want to tell you."

"Can it wait?" He stripped off his shirt, revealing his rock-hard chest and perfectly chiseled stomach. His tanned skin was tight, and every separation of muscle was obvious. His biceps were toned and defined, and there was a significant separation before his triceps began. He would be the perfect inspiration for a sculpture of a Greek god. His belt was undone, and then his pants came next. He stood in his boxers then moved into me, one hand sliding into my hair while the other wrapped around my waist. "Right now, all I want to do is fuck." He wrapped my hair around his knuckles and gave the back of my head a gentle tug, forcing my gaze to meet his.

My hands moved up his hard body, my fingers exploring the crevasses between his muscles. "It can wait…but I don't think you want to wait."

His chocolate eyes penetrated mine, and his heated gaze quickly turned into an unbridled forest fire. "Then tell me." His hand slid down my jeans until he gripped my ass. He gave me a tight squeeze, showing how powerful he was with just a single hand.

"I want to take your last name."

For less than an instant, his eyes softened. His grip on my hair relaxed for just a second before it tightened again. His gaze turned more intense than it was just a second ago. Now he seemed more aggressive, fueled by my revelation. "You want to be Mrs. Hunt?"

"Yes…more than anything."

My words made him snap, and he yanked me harder as he covered my mouth with his. He kissed me harshly, nearly bruising my lips and making them throb. The beast inside the man had been released, and now he handled me like a prize rather than a woman. His ancestral caveman ways rose to the surface, and he maneuvered me backward as he directed me toward the hallway.

He scooped me into his arms and carried me by the ass into the bedroom we shared. He dropped me on the mattress instead of gently laying me down, and he yanked off my clothes without any care. He dragged my hips to the edge of the bed then separated my thighs by gripping the backs of my knees.

He pointed his dick into my entrance then gave a harsh thrust, shoving his big dick inside me without giving me a chance to prepare. He dug his fingers into my flesh and let out a moan filled with testosterone.

It felt good, but the quick intrusion was also painful. No matter how many times he fucked me, my petiteness would never be able to handle his dick moving so aggressively. I would always need time to adjust, to stretch for his size.

But right now, he didn't care.

He fucked me just the way he did the first time we hooked up. It was rough, hard, and fast. He pulled me harder into him and locked his gaze on mine, enjoying the sight of me as my tits shook with the thrust.

My hands locked around his wrists, and I enjoyed the fullness of his cock. He stretched me well, so now his size was only pleasurable. He moved through my slickness and was coated in it, our mutual arousal rubbing together as our body parts feasted on each other.

He moved his hands on either side of my waist and leaned over me, deepening the angle so his cock hit me deep with every thrust. One hand migrated into my hair then grabbed the back of my neck. He tugged on me as he slammed into me, his cock moving even harder. "Mine."

Both of my hands gripped his forearms as I moaned in his face. I allowed him to take me, to claim all of me. I yielded my control and fear completely, giving him the trust and love I hadn't been able to give anyone for a decade. I became the most vulnerable I'd ever been, surrendering to a man who had earned my unflinching loyalty. It was the most freeing sensation I'd ever known, to ache for his possessiveness rather than fear it. I wanted this man to dominate me, trusted him to do it right. In the end, Diesel Hunt won. I folded and crowned him the victor. "Yours."

———

We skipped dinner and chose to stay in bed.

We'd take breaks in between, curling up together under the sheets. Then a simple touch would turn into a caress, an innocent kiss would be full of tongue, and then he was on top of me again, sinking me into the mattress with his size and burying his cock between my legs. He fucked me in the same position over and over, my small body pinned underneath his. He kept stuffing me with his come, making it drip back out onto the sheets beneath me.

The room smelled like sex.

After the fourth round, he pulled me against his body and hooked my leg over his hip. He glided his hand up my leg, gently touching my skin with his fingertips until he reached my hip. Then he slid down the curve of my waist toward my chest. His thumb flicked over my nipples before he went back the other way. He touched me like he'd never had the opportunity before. His deep voice interrupted the silence between us. "What made you change your mind?"

"A few things…"

"Such as?" he pressed.

"Your father said something to me the other day, saying I should consider your request romantic. But it was mostly Thorn who made me see things differently."

He grinned. "I knew he'd come through for me."

"He said his opinions are his own."

"Of course. He wouldn't lie to you. His loyalty is to you, not me."

"He reminded me that you've always been loyal to me, that you've loved me from the beginning. You earned my trust, and you're the man I love. I should give you something I've never given anyone else before, so that's why I decided to do it. You're going to be my husband…you should have all of me."

He released a moan so quiet I wasn't sure if I heard it or just imagined it. He gripped my hip tightly, his fingers digging into me. "I couldn't agree with him more."

"I want to wear your name. I want the world to know I'm yours. I also want the world to know you're mine."

"That we belong to each other," he whispered.

"It's hard to let go of my identity and embrace a new one...but it's a good thing. I want to be a Hunt. I want to share an empire with you. I want to be partners with you, the truest and deepest kind."

"That makes me very happy. You have no idea."

"It makes me happy too. I'm sorry I was so difficult about it."

"Don't apologize," he said. "I understand. You made the right decision, and that's all that matters." His hand moved up my neck before it cupped my cheek. His fingers dug gently into the fall of my hair, and he stared at me with his deep brown eyes. "I hope that means you've surrendered yourself to me."

"I have...I trust you."

He pressed his forehead to mine then placed a kiss there. "The second you wear my last name, I'm not going to be the same guy. I'll be more intense, more aggressive. I'll be territorial, a little crazy. I hope you accept that."

"I expect nothing less."

He kissed me on the mouth. "Then marry me now."

# CHAPTER EIGHT

THORN

We sat across from each other in the conference room, the damn glass doors surrounding us on all sides. I wasn't a big fan of professionalism, so perhaps being fish in a bowl was a good way to keep me in line.

Autumn did a great job of pretending we were just colleagues. She stuck to work, discussing when the first product line would be in full effect and how it should be distributed. While she was a scientist, she was knowledgeable about her business margins. She knew the company inside and out, which was impressive because she probably dedicated most of her time to the lab.

She closed her folders when our discussion came to an end. "You aren't very talkative today."

"You're distracting."

"I'm distracting you from work when I'm talking about work?" she asked incredulously.

"I'm not really listening to you. I'm just looking at you."

She rolled her eyes, but her slight smile suggested she liked the attention. "What happened to being professional?"

"Do you see me grabbing your ass?"

"No. But I suspect if this big table weren't in between us, things would be different…"

"Actually, it's the glass doors." I nodded to the wall behind me. "I don't know why Titan is so obsessed with being transparent. Annoying."

"She wants the world to know she has nothing to hide."

Secrets were underrated.

"I guess I should get back to my lab." She gathered her documents and placed them in her satchel. She pulled it over her shoulder, the dark blue leather bag complimenting the black dress she wore. She was in sky-high heels, and I assumed she must change out of them when she was working in the lab.

I rose to my feet and came around the desk, blocking her exit. "Let's have dinner tonight."

"Dinner, huh?" she asked. "Will you be cooking?"

"If you want. I was gonna pick up something."

"That's not bad either."

"I don't want to spend any more time in the kitchen than necessary when I have better things to do…" I was already undressing her with my eyes, imagining the feeling of her lace panties scrunched up in my fist.

"Do I qualify as something better to do?"

"If you don't know, I'll show you later." I stepped out of the way so she could get to the door, but if our walls weren't see-through, I'd be kissing her on the mouth right now. My hands would be palming her ass and squeezing it tight.

She smiled then walked to the door. "I look forward to it, Thorn." She pushed the door open and walked down the hallway.

I watched her hips shake as she moved, saw the way her calves tightened with every step she took. I still had hours to get through before I finally had her underneath me. That time couldn't come soon enough.

———

Her black hair was in loose curls, smoky makeup was on her face, and she wore a sweater dress that was so tight it didn't leave much to the imagination.

She dressed up—just for me.

I was a king.

My hands immediately lifted up her dress and kneaded her bare ass with my fingertips. She had on brown booties, but the rest of her legs were bare, tanned skin that was about to be the victim of my aggressive lips. My face lingered in front of hers, but I didn't move in for the kiss, as much as I wanted to.

I teased her.

I brushed my nose against hers and looked into her

vibrant eyes. She had the energy of an entire forest, pure and beautiful. There was something about this woman that stood out compared to all the others. Some names I couldn't even remember, but Autumn was a name I'd never forget. Her specialness wasn't just a derivative of her looks. Combined with the smile, that sassy intellect, and the way she carried herself, she was the most desirable woman on the planet.

I squeezed her ass tighter as I held her in my doorway. I had dinner on the table, but now I wasn't thinking about food.

"Are you going to kiss me or what?" She spoke with a sultry voice, seducing me with the way her words grazed over my skin.

"No. Not until you beg me." I moved my mouth against the shell of her ear, smelling the scent of her lovely hair, and I kissed the skin just below her ear, making sure she heard the way my lips brushed against her.

The fiery look in her eyes told me it had the right effect.

I grabbed her by the hand and pulled her to the table. "Rib eye steak, potatoes, and broccoli."

Like she was in a drug-infused haze, it took her a minute to come back to reality. "How do you look so good if you eat like this all the time?"

"I don't eat like this all the time. Just when I'm trying to impress a lady."

She sat down and immediately sipped her wine. "I thought you said you didn't cook for anyone?"

"I don't. You're the first lady I've actually tried to impress."

She smiled but maintained a guarded expression at the same time. "Is that a line?"

"I already have you, Autumn. Why would I need a line?" I laid the napkin across my lap and picked up my fork.

She took a longer drink from her glass before she set it down. "Then why do you want to impress me, Thorn?"

"I like you."

"That's it?" she asked. "Because you've already impressed me in the way that matters most."

I didn't have to invite her over for dinner or spend time with her. With the others, we just had sex, and then they left. There was no meal or wine. I didn't notice how differently I was behaving until she pointed it out. "I'm not sure, honestly. With the other women I've been with, I don't ask them to dinner or really talk to them much. It's just right down to business."

"So Titan is the only relationship you've ever had?"

"I guess…" I drank my wine, feeling guilty for telling the lie.

"And the others were just…what we are?"

"I was never monogamous with any of them. They were just fun ways to spend my time. They liked my power and wealth, and they liked the things I did to them. Some of them were open to threesomes. Some were even open to four. I wouldn't compare those experiences to anything we have."

"Because we're only seeing each other?"

"Yeah. And because I actually like you."

"What do you like about me?"

"Everything," I said with a laugh. "You're the coolest woman I've ever met."

"Really?" she asked with a smile. "I've always thoughts scientists were labeled as uncool."

"Only uncool people say that."

She chuckled then cut into her steak. "Wow, this is good."

"My favorite place."

"I'll remember that. I'll pick you up a steak if I want to butter you up."

"You could save yourself the trip and just get on your knees instead."

She was about to take a bite of her food, but she narrowed her eyes on my face instead. "I thought the best way to a man was through food."

"I'm more of a sex kinda guy."

"I'll remember that."

"What about you?" I asked. "Sex or food?"

"Depends."

"On?"

"The guy. If it were sex with you or food, I'd pick sex. If it were sex with another guy…I'd probably pick food."

I stopped eating because this woman amazed me. She complimented me so many ways I could hardly believe it. It was like she was doing it on purpose…only she wasn't. "You're amazing."

"Amazing?" she asked.

"You know how to make me feel good."

Her cheeks slightly filled with color. "Just being honest…"

We returned to eating our meal, our chatter dying down after the last thing she said. The biggest thing we had in common was our work together, but ironically, I didn't think about it when we were together. Work was the last thing on my mind. I was far more interested in the woman than the partnership.

When we were finished, we left our plates on the table.

"Need help with the dishes?" she asked.

"No. The maid will take care of it."

"When does the maid come?"

"In the morning when I'm at work."

"Now, that makes sense. I thought it was strange your apartment was so clean."

"Hey." My hands moved to her hips, and I gave her a slight tickle. "Don't be like that, baby."

"Baby?" she asked, her stomach tightening against my fingertips.

"Yeah." It was the first time I'd ever called a woman that, but I liked it. I liked giving her a possessive nick-name, a name no one else called her. It made me feel closer to her, made it seem like she was mine even if she wasn't. "Is that okay?"

Her hands moved up my chest, and she rose on her tiptoes so she could look at me better. Her eyes trained on my lips, asking for a kiss without actually saying the words. Her fingertips dug into my t-shirt, like she wanted to yank it over my head. She rubbed her nose against mine but didn't lean in for the embrace. "Kiss me."

"I'll take that as a yes…"

"Then don't make me beg any longer."

———

I don't know how it happened, but we ended up on the rug in front of my gas fireplace in the living room. With my arms pinned behind her knees as I held all my weight on top of her, I fucked her into the floor.

"Fuck…" The sight of her tits, her slender waistline, and the sexy expressions she made as I pleased her made this feel more like a wet dream than reality. It was too good to be true. My cock could feel the cream her pussy made for me, the slickness of arousal. I'd already fucked her twice, but now my cock was buried inside her for the third time that night. "Your pussy…Jesus." I was hot and sticky because of the sweat, but that didn't slow me down. I pushed through my own come and felt it drip down my balls. I kept giving it to her, but her tiny pussy couldn't take all of it, not when I was ramming my big cock inside her.

Autumn had been lost in me since we started. She'd come around my cock more times than she ever had before, and her warm hands continued to claw at me. I knew she cut through the skin because my sweat burned when it seeped into the wounds. She'd be sore tomorrow morning, but right now, all she felt was the pleasure I gave her.

She ran her hands up my chest then gripped my shoulders as her hair stretched out behind her on the rug. Her cheeks were pink, and her eyes were brighter than the northern lights. Her tits shook with my thrusts, and her nipples remained hard for the entire duration. I could feel her pussy constrict around my dick every time she came.

Fuck, this was the best sex I'd ever had.

And she just lay there. That's how sexy she was.

"I never want to stop fucking you…"

Her hand gripped the back of my neck, and she pulled my mouth to hers for a kiss. "Then don't."

I felt her breath enter my mouth along with her words. My cock twitched inside her, slathered in my own come and hers. I wanted to keep going, but when this woman told me to never stop fucking her, I couldn't control my load.

I came inside her for the third time that night, pumping my seed deep inside her tight pussy. I groaned as the satisfaction trickled up my spine. My balls tightened toward my body and gave me an extra rush of goodness. "So fucking good…"

She rubbed her hand up my chest and to my neck, the same look of satisfaction in her eyes.

I grabbed her hand and turned it to expose her wrist. I pressed a kiss against the sensitive skin, my eyes connected with hers. I'd never been with a woman who made me feel this good. No threesome or foursome compared to having my dick inside this woman. There wasn't necessarily anything special about the sex, but there was something special about her. "I want to keep going, but I need a break this time…"

"You're worth the wait." She sat up and kissed my chest, running her tongue along my sweat and catching the drops.

My hand fisted her hair as I cradled her head toward me. "Sleep over."

"Tonight?" she asked.

"Yeah." I didn't invite women to spend the night with me, but I knew I would start my day off right with some morning sex. "I didn't ask. I'm telling you that you're spending the night."

"Not sure why you think I respond well to orders."

"You don't." I tilted her head back and looked into her eyes. "But you respond to me."

I knew it was the right answer when a soft smile stretched across her face. "I have to warn you, I snore."

"Don't care."

"And I hog the blankets."

"I'm usually too hot anyway."

"And I may unexpectedly ride you in the middle of the night."

I grinned. "Even better." I was still inside her, but my dick had softened throughout our exchange. I could feel my warm come surround me because I was still buried deep inside her. I leaned down and kissed her, enjoying the taste of her lips in front of the quiet fireplace. My hand dug into her hair, and I felt the rush of excitement when she agreed to stay with me.

I'd have her all night.

The intercom on my elevator beeped. Then Titan spoke. "Hey, Diesel and I are coming up. Is that okay?"

My lips stopped in mid-kiss as disappointment rushed through me. It was the first time Titan was out of the house, and while that excited me, she couldn't have picked a worse time.

Autumn pulled her lips away, her face full of surprise at the sound of Titan's voice.

Ugh, I hated Titan right now.

I pulled out of Autumn quickly and walked to the elevator with my dick still wet. I pressed my hand to the button and tried not to sound like a complete dick. "Hey, guys. What's up?"

"We have some great news we wanted to share with you," Titan said. "We're coming up."

"Whoa, hold on." I watched Autumn climb to her feet and pull on her clothes. I didn't want her to hide somewhere like a dirty secret, but I also didn't want to tell Titan to leave because she probably had something important to say. "Just give me a second, alright? The place is a mess."

"Since when did you start caring?" Titan asked with a laugh.

"Just hold on." I left the intercom and walked up to Autumn. "I would just tell them to leave, but they wouldn't stop by unless it was important. I haven't seen Titan leave her place in over a month, so this is probably big."

"That's okay," she said. "I understand."

I thought she was taking this surprisingly well. "Well, just wait in my bedroom until they leave. I'll try to get them out fast."

"Whoa, what?" After she flicked her hair back, she stared at me with fiery green eyes. "You want me to hide?"

"If she sees you here, she's going to know what we were doing."

"And does it matter if she does?" She crossed her arms over her chest. "Are you embarrassed by me or something?"

"Are you kidding me?" I countered. "Look at you. Hell no, I'm not embarrassed."

"Then why is this a secret? You didn't tell her we were seeing each other?"

"No. I thought that would be unprofessional."

"How so?" she asked. "You used to sleep with Titan.

Why can't you sleep with me? You're only helping her temporarily."

"I thought you wouldn't want me to tell her," I argued. "A gentleman doesn't blab about his conquests to people."

"But I thought she was your friend?"

"Of course she is." This was turning into a nightmare, and the time was ticking. "She told me not to get involved with you since she's doing business with you. She told me that after I was already seeing you…so now I don't know what to do. I don't want to drop this bomb on her right this second."

"Why would she tell you not to see me?"

"Conflict of interest, I guess."

"So you told her you wanted to see me?"

Titan spoke through the intercom again. "Thorn? Everything alright?"

Autumn continued to stare at me suspiciously.

"Can we finish this conversation after they leave?" I asked. "I'm not happy about this and I feel like an ass, but I don't know what else to do. Cut me some slack."

She pulled on her shoes then snatched her clutch off the table. Then she walked down the hallway and entered my bedroom.

Fuck, my perfect night was ruined.

I pulled on my clothes then hit the button. "Come up." I dragged my hands down my face and tried to fight the migraine that started behind my eyes. The last thing I wanted to do was push Autumn away. I wanted to share my bed with her and enjoy her tomorrow morning. If Titan and Diesel weren't family to me, I would tell them to get lost.

The elevator doors opened a moment later, and they stepped inside.

Titan was in great shape. She was dressed nicely, she was smiling, and her hand was held in Diesel's.

"It's nice to be outside again, huh?" I asked with a laugh.

"It's nice to get out of the house," Titan said. "I haven't felt fresh air in so long."

"And it's nice of you to let her get out of the house." I shook Diesel's hand.

"I think it's time." The second he dropped my hand, he returned it around her waist.

"We hope we aren't interrupting anything," Titan said.

"No, don't worry about it." I hoped they wouldn't notice the empty dishes on the kitchen table or pick up on the obvious odor of sex from the living room. I didn't invite them to the couches because I was trying to keep them away from the opposite side of the penthouse. I didn't want Autumn to overhear something she shouldn't. "So, do you have any big news?"

"Yes," Titan said. "We're finally getting married."

"Yeah?" I asked. "When?"

"It's kinda short notice but…next weekend."

"That's not bad," I said. "You know I'll be there. Where?"

"Thailand," Diesel answered. "It's a far trip, but we're only inviting about a dozen people."

"Oh, I love Thailand. You know I'm down for that." It was a beautiful country with gorgeous beaches. I'd been there a few times. "I'm excited for you guys. This has been a long time coming, and now it's finally happening."

"We're very excited about it." Titan shared an affectionate look with Diesel.

Diesel mirrored her gaze. "Thank you for encouraging her to take my last name. Best gift she could have ever given me."

"I didn't have to do much convincing." I slid my hands into the pockets of my jeans. "She'd always wanted it. I just had to make her realize how much."

"Thank you anyway," Diesel said. "I'm counting down the days until I can call her Mrs. Hunt." When he turned his gaze on her, he rubbed his nose against hers.

It reminded me of Autumn for some reason. "Thanks for stopping by to tell me in person. I'll hunt for my swim trunks after you leave."

"There's one other thing." Titan stepped away from Diesel and came toward me, and judging by the affection in her eyes, she had something to ask me. Her look was full of emotion before she even said anything. "Thorn...you know what I'm going to ask you."

Yeah, I did. "And you know what my answer is going to be."

"You'll give me away?" she asked. "There's no one else I want more."

The media wouldn't be able to comprehend why we would do such a thing. Would I really give away my ex-fiancée to her new lover? It didn't sound plausible. But I knew this was important to her because our relationship was so much deeper than anyone realized. "I'd be honored."

"Thank you." She moved into my chest and hugged me. "You're the closest thing to family that I have."

"I know." I held her back. "You're my family too."

She stayed there for a while, holding me longer than she ever had before.

When Diesel watched us, there was a hint of jealousy there. I was the last man he should be jealous of, considering she backed out of marrying me. The love between us was purely familial. Just because it wasn't romantic didn't mean it wasn't deep.

She pulled away and regarded me with the same emotional eyes. "You've always been so good to me. Even when I broke our arrangement because I fell in love, you still came back to me."

I hoped Autumn didn't hear that. "It'll always be you and me. The only difference now is we also have Diesel…so there's three of us."

"Yeah…we're a family. You've been my best friend for ten years. And I know we'll be best friends forever."

I didn't say anything because I was scared to egg her on. I needed to tell Autumn the truth, but I wanted to be the one to tell her. And I needed to talk to Titan about it first. "Of course."

She moved back to Diesel. "I'm going to get my dress tomorrow. You want to come along and help me out?"

Dress shopping wasn't my thing, but I couldn't say no. "Sure."

"Make sure she picks out a good once," Diesel said. "The more skin, the better."

"I'll try," I said with a chuckle.

They said their goodbyes and then left my penthouse. When the elevator doors were closed and they were finally gone, I headed to my bedroom and hoped I'd find Autumn in a better mood than when I left her.

When I saw her face, I realized my wish hadn't come true.

"She wants you to give her away?" she asked incredulously.

I knew this was going to be bad. "Her father passed away when she was young."

"I know that, but I think that's strange… You don't?" She cocked an eyebrow.

No, she was right. It was strange. "I—"

"I wondered if she was still in love with you, and then when I heard that, it makes me think she must be… I can't think of any other explanation for that."

She was so far off she was in an entirely different galaxy.

"I've always admired Titan because of the smart

and savvy businesswoman she is. She wouldn't be where she is today unless she was a genius. But all of this confuses me. She either still has feelings for you, or she's totally insensitive by asking you to give her away. I mean, that's just rude. To even expect you to be at the wedding…is cold."

Now that Titan's image was taking a hit, I couldn't let this go on any longer. I didn't want Autumn to question her business relationship with Titan. If she pulled out of the deal, it would hurt Titan considerably. "We need to talk…" I sat on the edge on the edge of my bed and patted the seat beside me.

She eyed it warily before she sat. "What is it, Thorn?"

"What I'm about to say is going to confuse you… but I'm telling the truth. I don't want you thinking Titan is some kind of emotional psychopath, so I need to come clean. But I really hope you keep this between us."

"Okay…" She crossed her legs on the bed and rested her hands in her lap.

Something in my chest told me I could trust Autumn. She wouldn't betray Titan's secret to the world. It would hurt Titan as well as me. We'd look like the biggest liars on the planet. "Titan and I never had a real relationship. She and I have been friends for over a decade now, and she'd come to the realization that she didn't want to have a relationship with anyone. I didn't either. But she wanted to have a family, as did I. So we thought we would get married and have a family. Our relationship wouldn't be based on romance. It was an arrangement based on trust, loyalty, and honesty. She would be free to have her physical relationships, and I would have mine. But at the end of the day, we were committed to each other. I'd love her and protect her like any husband should, but I would never be in love with her." I stared across the room at the floor-to-ceiling windows that showed the city. Looking at Autumn's face didn't seem appealing, not when I dropped this heavy truth on her.

Judging by her silence, she didn't know what to say.

"She met Diesel before we got engaged. She fell in love with him, but they broke up over a misunderstanding. When they got back together, I had already proposed to her. She said she had to break it off. I was angry about it because she made me look like an idiot, but we managed to get through it. Now here we are… still friends." I turned to her to watch Autumn's reaction.

Her expression hadn't changed at all, but she opened her mouth slightly to speak. She closed it again and cleared her throat. "So…it was all a publicity stunt?"

"I guess. But we weren't doing it for the publicity."

"Did you guys ever…?"

"Not once. I've never even kissed her."

"But you could picture yourself spending your life with her?"

"As a partner, yes. Like I said before, I was never in love with her. I was happy when she met Diesel. He's a great guy. I know they'll be happy together for a very long time."

"Why did she agree to this arrangement? Titan is beautiful and successful…she could have any man she wanted."

I didn't want to betray Titan's secrets, but her history was a matter of public record now. "She was in an abusive relationship when she was young. Messed her up mentally and she had trust issues. She wanted to be with someone she could depend on, someone she could trust implicitly. She knew I would always look out for her, never raise a hand to her, and I could be everything she needed. I'd be a great father to her kids, and I come from a good family…all of that stuff. And then she could continue to have her physical relationships too. It was perfect for both of us."

"Why was it perfect for you?"

"I didn't want a relationship either. Having Titan as a wife solved my problems. It made my parents happy. Financially, it was a good move. I enjoy her company and trust her with my life. True friends that will always remain loyal to you are hard to find…especially in a cruel world like this."

She crossed her arms over her chest, pulling the dress tighter against her body. She must have fixed her hair with her fingertips while I was in the living room with Diesel and Titan because it looked nice again.

I waited in silence, practically walking on eggshells. "Autumn?"

She cleared her throat. "I'm sure you and Titan aren't the first ones to make an arrangement like that... but I'm just caught off guard. I told you stuff about my personal life because I thought you would understand... I feel a little stupid now."

"No, don't feel stupid." My hand gripped hers. "Please."

She wouldn't look at me.

"Baby."

She fought the nickname initially, but after ten seconds, she finally turned to me.

"I don't want you to feel that way. I feel guilty because I misled you, but I'm glad you shared that with me. I feel like I know you better because of that...and I feel closer to you."

"I told you something honest and personal about myself. Now I want to know something about you."

"Anything. What do you want to know?"

"What is the real reason you don't want a relationship?"

I didn't want to sugarcoat the truth. She told me something that was difficult to share, and it would be insulting if I didn't expose my truth to her. "I just don't feel anything. I've been with a lot of women, but I've never come close to falling in love with someone. I've never had my heart broken. I just like having meaningless flings, and I like being with women that allow me to control them…to do what I want." As the words left my lips, I knew I sounded like an asshole. She didn't want a relationship either, but at least it was for a legitimate reason.

Her expression didn't change, and she didn't seem to view me judgmentally.

"That doesn't mean I'm not a gentleman. It doesn't mean I'm not honest. It doesn't mean I don't care. Titan is the only woman I've had a close relationship with besides my mom. Titan's an incredible person, and obviously, she's beautiful…but I've never felt anything. It makes me wonder if I'm incapable of feeling romantic love. Maybe there's something wrong with me, I'm not sure. When I see the way Diesel looks at Titan, I know I've never looked at anyone that way."

"Thank you for telling me."

"I know how that makes me sound…but I hope that doesn't chase you off."

"It doesn't," she said simply. "But I'm not sure if your assessment of yourself is completely accurate."

"How so?"

She tucked her hair behind her and took her gaze off mine. "Maybe I'm going out on a limb here…but I feel like you care about me."

"Of course I do." I knew I did. I couldn't get enough of her. I'd never asked a woman to stay over before. I'd never cooked for someone before.

"But, I think you care about me differently than you do with other women."

"Why do you say that?"

"You've never made dinner for someone. You've never had anyone sleep over. It just seems like…maybe I'm different."

I'd never given it much thought. I hadn't been seeing her that long.

"You're a very jealous man…I know that much." She chuckled.

"Yeah…you're right."

"You're the one who wanted to be monogamous."

That was true too.

"Maybe you've grown. Maybe seeing Titan in love has influenced you."

"Yeah, I guess it's possible…but you don't want a relationship anyway, right?"

She looked down again, a smile on her face. "I mean, if I met a good guy I really trusted and it felt right…I'd keep an open mind."

Why did that make me happy? Why did that bring a smile to my face? I interlocked her fingers with mine then brought her hand to my lips. I rested my mouth there for a moment, treasuring her warm skin. "And if I met an amazing woman…I'd keep an open mind too."

———

I didn't know how Titan would react.

But I suspected she was going to be pissed.

I kinda lied to her about seeing Autumn, and then I

told Autumn the truth about my false relationship with Titan. It was a betrayal on a few accounts, but hopefully, she wouldn't care that much since she was getting married in less than two weeks.

Titan's driver drove us down the street toward the fashion designers' studios. I'd left the office a little earlier than usual so we'd have plenty of time to get the right dress. I suspected Connor Suede was making something just for her. "Does Connor know your ideas?"

"Connor?" Titan gave me a blank look. Back in elegant clothes with perfectly styled hair, she was back to her usual self. The only thing that was different was her feet. Now she wore flats instead of heels, still not quite strong enough to wear them on the slippery sidewalk after a long day of rain.

"He's designing your dress, right?"

"No," she said with a chuckle. "God, could you imagine the massacre?"

"I'm not following."

"Diesel knows I slept with him…so he's not a fan."

I nodded my head slowly. "Gotcha…"

"I'm going with Chase Cruz. He specializes in wedding dresses anyway. Connor's talents are better suited to office and resort clothes."

I was relieved I didn't have to see him. He wanted to fuck my woman, and I wasn't too happy about it. Of course, if he'd known I was seeing Autumn, he would have backed off because he was a gentleman, but his ignorance didn't make me hate him less. "Do you have any idea of what you want?"

"Yes. Mermaid fit but with lace sleeves. Something simple but elegant. And I want the back to be open. Diesel likes my back…" She smiled then looked out the window.

"TMI, Titan."

"You've told me worse things, Thorn. Don't act innocent."

I had mentioned my threesome on two sex swings. It was a graphic tale. "True." I wondered when I should tell her about Autumn and me. I was planning on doing it today because I couldn't keep it a secret anymore. While my personal life was none of her business, this pertained to her. "Thanks for bringing me along."

"Of course. According to Diesel's orders, you have to make sure I look hot."

I chuckled. "You always look hot, Titan. You could be dressed in one of those inflatable T-rex costumes and Diesel would still think you're stunning."

She smiled. "Yeah…you're probably right."

I'd never really noticed how happy she was when she talked about him. I knew she loved him, and I was aware enough to see their intense and passionate relationship. But the depth of their connection was deep and meaningful. Their story was written all across her face—and her heart.

Was Autumn right? Was there hope for me?

We arrived at the office and were escorted into the

design room. Chase Cruz greeted Titan with a kiss on each cheek then shook my hand. A handsome man that could model his own clothes if he wished, Chase Cruz spoke with a Puerto Rican accent that would floor any woman he tried to impress. "Lovely, as always. Thank you so much for allowing me to design your dress. Truly, it's an honor."

Titan patted his shoulder. "You're too sweet, Chase. I'm excited for you to make me beautiful."

"And I will," he said. "It'll be no challenge. Mr. Hunt is a lucky man." He handed her a nude slip, a thin material that would barely conceal her breasts if she wore it. "Put this on, and I'll get your measurements."

Titan walked into the changing room and shut the door.

I sat in a chair outside the room, a glass of champagne with a plate of chocolate covered strawberries beside it. It was an elegant touch, but I was more of a scotch-soaked fruit kinda guy. "I'm surprised Diesel let you out of the house today."

"He doesn't let me do anything, Thorn. Let's get that straight." Her voice grew quiet then loud as she removed clothes and pulled the slip over her head. "And he was comfortable with it because he knew you were coming along."

I'd already killed a man for her. What else wouldn't I do?

She came out in just the slip then stood on the platform in the center of the room. The dress covered everything, but it was still showing most of her skin. I directed my gaze to my phone to give her some privacy.

Chase took her measurements all over her body then pulled out different dresses to see what she liked. All the big puffy ones were rejected, and the simple ones were the clear winners. Together, they examined the lacework and determined what Titan liked the most.

"What about diamonds?" Chase asked. "Real diamonds?"

"No," she said. "I want the only diamond to be the one on my finger."

Chase nodded in understanding. "Then I think the lace would be better. I could do simple sleeves, open in the back, and I'll have it fitted perfectly against the small of your back. You have natural curves, and it'll make the dress seem like a second skin."

"That sounds perfect."

"It'll take me some time, but if I start today, I should have it done in a week."

"Thank you, Chase. I know I'm asking for a lot."

"For Tatum Titan, anything."

She kept her smile, but her eyes slightly crinkled with a hint of sadness.

Soon, no one would call her by that name ever again.

———

We returned to her penthouse, and Titan showed me

the suit she wanted me to wear. It was my favorite designer, and it was a color I'd worn many times. But since this was her day, I didn't care what she asked me to wear.

I even would have worn a clown suit if she asked.

"What do you think?" she asked.

"I like it." It was navy blue with a black tie. "What will Diesel be wearing?"

"Black suit."

"So I'll be the only one in blue?"

"Yep." She pulled the plastic back over the suit and laid it over the back of the couch. "I had my assistant make most of the arrangements. I got you one of their best suites at the resort. Will you be taking a date?"

The thought hadn't crossed my mind. The only person I would take was Autumn, but I couldn't blurt that out right this second. "I'm not sure yet. So…who is all invited?"

"Just some of my friends, Diesel's family, and a few other people."

"How about Ms. Alexander? You don't know her that well, but you guys will probably be good friends eventually."

"I'm not sure," she said. "It's a tricky situation, and I haven't made up my mind yet."

I might make it up for her.

"You want anything to drink?" she asked as she walked into the kitchen.

"I'll have whatever you're having." I took a seat on the couch beside my suit.

"I can still only have water," she called back. "So are you sure about that?"

I cringed. "Give me a single malt."

She grabbed her glass and made my drink at the bar before she returned. "I'm not sure if I've ever seen you drink water since I've known you…"

"Because I don't," I teased.

"I can imagine how your conversations go with your doctor…"

"Not well," I said with a chuckle. I took a long drink, feeling the burn down my throat and all the way into my stomach. The heat followed immediately afterward, giving me a jolt of energy to push through this. "Titan, I've got something to tell you. I'm gonna be up front with you…you aren't going to like it."

She crossed her legs and set her glass on the table. "Too bad I can't have an Old Fashioned to prepare for it." She leaned forward and rested her arms on her knee. "What is it, Thorn? And please tell me it has nothing to do with Diesel."

"Actually, it doesn't."

She sighed in relief. "Well, that makes it a little easier, I guess."

I rubbed my palms together and tried to find the right sentence to start with, but there wasn't a good option.

Titan looked at me expectantly.

I felt her hard gaze. "I'm sleeping with Autumn." Now it was out in the open. My secret was no longer a secret, and it actually felt good to get off my chest. "It started almost a month ago." I avoided her gaze because I already knew what her expression would look like.

She was pissed. "Since before I made her a partner?"

I nodded. "I went to her office to negotiate your terms, and…the attraction was there. Every time I was around her, it kept building. Then we were both at a party, and she made a move on me." I didn't tell her the specifics, that Autumn stared at my package without shame and became a big admirer of my dick.

When Titan sighed, I knew she was livid. She wasn't the kind of person who screamed her head off when she was angry. Her silence was sharper than a steak knife. It cut through the air with the sting of salt on an open wound. "This is unbelievable…I can't believe you didn't tell me."

"I don't need to tell you every single detail of my personal life, Titan." I rounded on her, reminding her that we had our own lives despite how close we were. "I didn't want you to think less of her because she wanted to sleep with me."

"I don't care about what you do with your dick, Thorn. But I relied on you to tell me if she was a good fit for the company. You were my eyes and ears. And now I find out your objectivity was compromised because you were screwing her the entire time. I trusted you."

This was something I wasn't prepared for. I didn't even realize she would feel that way until she said it, and now I realized it was a legitimate concern. "My objectivity was never compromised. Autumn is a humble genius. You couldn't find anyone better. And frankly, you couldn't compete against her. This was the only option."

She jumped to her feet then started pacing across the room, her arms crossed over her chest. "You didn't tell me to protect her privacy, but you didn't protect my goals. Your allegiance should have been to me, Thorn. Not her. And you really think I would judge a woman for wanting to sleep with a man? Come on, you must not know me at all." She shook her head and released another sigh.

"I thought it would be a one-time thing, so I didn't think I needed to tell you that."

"And when did it stop being a one-time thing?"

Immediately. "I can't recall."

She stopped walking and glared at me.

When I had Autumn once, I wanted her again. I knew it the second I fucked her. "A few days afterward…"

"So this became a relationship?"

"Not a relationship. An arrangement. She didn't want a relationship, and neither did I…but we didn't want to see other people either."

"Which makes it a relationship," she snapped. "If it were a one-time thing, it probably wouldn't matter. But you actually know this woman. You share thoughts and feelings. It clouds your ability to make valid decisions. You could have pushed for it just because of your infatuation."

"Give me more credit than that, Titan." I stood up and started to pace. "I'm not some idiot that will fall for anything a woman will say. I can keep things separate. I know she's the perfect partner for you, and regardless of what happens between us, that will never change. That's not just a gut instinct. That's a claim backed up by evidence."

Titan shifted her weight to one leg, her arms crossed and the fiery look still in her eyes. She tapped her fingers against her arm as she considered what I said. I knew she was thinking because of the focused look on her face. She was debating with herself, going over everything that was said with a critical approach. "In the end, it doesn't change anything. This is where we are now, and we have to make the best of it...I suppose."

"It'll be great, Titan. Autumn is the supergenius you need to rise to the next level."

"I sincerely hope you're right." She finally looked at me again, calm but irritated.

We'd gotten through the first obstacle. Hopefully, we'd get through the next one. "There's something else..."

She sighed in preparation.

"We'd been spending a lot of time together, and she believed the romance you and I had. It came up a lot, and she told me something very personal about herself because of it. Her opinion of you started to change because she couldn't understand why you would ask me to give you away...or why you want me at your wedding at all. She kept evaluating the situation critically and couldn't come up with a better explanation other than you're a sadist and a psychopath...so I told her the truth."

Now she let out a growl. "You've got to be kidding me."

I slid my hands into my pockets and shrugged. "I didn't have any other choice."

"Yes, you did," she snapped. "You could have just not said anything."

"Titan, you were the one taking the hit to your reputation. It would have affected your working relationship with her."

"Which never would have happened in the first place if you hadn't started fucking her." Now the fire couldn't be put out, and she was livid. She'd kept her calmness for the first part of the conversation, but all civility was out the window. "Thorn, you can have any other woman in this damn city."

"Well, I don't want anyone else."

As if a bucket of water had been dumped over her head, the blazing fire was immediately snuffed out.

"I understand why you're upset, and it was a stupid decision on my part. But you accepted my engagement and made me look like a damn idiot to the entire world. I still get strange looks when I go out."

Her eyes immediately fell in guilt.

"So this makes us even. You fucked up, and now I fucked up. Truce?"

She lowered her hands to her sides, her sigh accompanying the disappearance of anger. "Truce."

Never thought I'd be happy that she screwed me over in front of the entire world, but now it had paid off. I just cashed in my get-out-of-jail-free card. But that was my one lifeline. It couldn't have been better sent.

"Correct me if I'm wrong, but it sounds like you actually like this woman."

"I do like her."

She stepped closer to me, treating me with the softness she showed earlier that day when we designed her wedding dress. "You know what I mean? I've never heard you say you like someone. You usually just like her ass or something."

"I do like Autumn's ass...but I like everything else too."

Titan stared at me with that knowing gaze, looking right through me like an X-ray machine. "Is she the real deal?"

"I don't know, Titan. Right now, all I know is I like being with her, and I want to keep seeing her."

"Monogamously?" She cocked an eyebrow.

"Yes."

Her eyebrow relaxed, but her smile widened. "This is a first."

"I'll probably get bored with her like I do with everyone else. But for now, I'm happy where I am."

She returned to her seat on the couch and grabbed her water. "If I could, I'd be having a long drink with you. The water will have to do. So tell me all the details."

"Come on, I don't kiss and tell."

She almost choked on her water when she laughed. "No, all you ever do is kiss and tell."

"But not in a situation like this. You work with her. It's inappropriate."

"Thorn, I'm your best friend. You tell me about all the others."

"The others are different."

"Because?"

"I don't care about them."

As if she'd just discovered a piece of gold no one else noticed just yet, she smiled. "I guess that's everything I need to know…"

"Don't get your hopes up."

"Too late."

"Because nothing has changed."

"Everything has changed. The second you stopped wearing a condom, the second you didn't confide the details to your best friend, and the second you told me about her was the moment it became different. But different isn't a bad thing, Thorn. I always hoped you would find someone just like I have. There's no greater feeling in the world."

I saw the way they looked at each other almost every day. I saw the unflinching loyalty they had for each other. I saw their love grow as the year passed, their love deepening and never shaking despite the obstacles in their way. Anyone who found that kind of love was very lucky.

But would I be one of them?

"I'm going to give you some advice, and you better take it."

"I didn't ask for any," I countered.

"Too bad, you're going to listen to me."

I rolled my eyes. "Advice from a woman who's been in one relationship her entire life…"

"One phenomenal relationship," she said. "And this is my advice. Be honest with her."

"Titan, when am I not honest? I give it so straight it makes people dislike me."

"Not honest in that way."

"Then what way?" I finished the rest of my whiskey before I wiped my mouth.

"Be honest about what the way you feel." She placed her hand over her heart. "Don't downplay your feelings. Don't tell her you want to see other people if you don't. Don't tell her you aren't into it just because you're scared. Put it all out there."

I looked away and didn't respond to her statement.

Titan wanted the best for me, so she turned optimistic. She didn't want me to be alone for the rest of my life, not that I wanted to either. "I was actually thinking about asking her something else…"

"What?" Titan asked.

"I was thinking about asking her if she wanted to have the same arrangement you and I had…"

"Why would she agree to that?"

"Because she wants the good stuff that goes with it, but not all the bad."

"Or you could just try to have something real…"

"And maybe we will…but maybe we could do it in a different way. She's afraid to get hurt, and I want some security. I'm getting older, and I want to have a partner. What better partner than a woman you're doing business with. She has a lot to offer, and she would be a great person to join my holdings with. And with kids… she'd make some beautiful ones."

"I guess I see what you mean."

"And maybe we'll fall in love on the way…maybe we won't. But no matter what, we'll be left with a relationship based on friendship, trust, and loyalty. And those are things that always last longer than love."

## CHAPTER NINE

VINCENT

The elevator doors opened, and I stepped inside the penthouse Tatum and my son occupied together. Now that they were getting married in a little over a week, I suspected some things would change.

But others would stay the same.

Nothing made me happier than seeing the way Tatum crossed the room so easily to hug me. She hugged me with a tight squeeze, not flinching from the pain in her chest. She seemed to be back to perfect health, so strong that it didn't seem like she'd been shot in the first place. Tragedies like the one she endured usually changed people.

It didn't change her at all.

"You look lovely, Tatum." When I pulled away, I glanced down at her ring. I used to see Isabella wear it every single day, but then it disappeared into the black hole of my nightstand. To see it on Tatum's hand brought me different kind of joy. It made it feel like Isabella was still here, welcoming in the daughter she never got to meet.

"Thanks, Vincent. Can I get you anything?"

"Just some water will be fine."

Titan retrieved a glass from the kitchen and carried it to the coffee table. "How have you been?"

"Making arrangements at work for my vacation time."

"I hope the wedding isn't too much of an inconvenience to you."

"Not at all." I sat on the couch, opening my coat button as I bent my body to sit. "I just have to be prepared. I work so I can have a life. I don't live to work. Big difference."

"And an important difference." She had a glass of water herself, but she didn't take a drink. Her lips were painted with her usual lipstick and she was in a black dress she would normally wear to the office, but she hadn't returned to work—to the best of my knowledge. "So, were you planning on bringing a date?" she asked. "So I can notify the wedding planner?"

I immediately broke eye contact, Scarlet's beautiful face coming into my mind. Her dark hair framed her face perfectly, and the slender lines of her neck made me want to kiss her everywhere. A week had come and gone, and I hadn't spoken to her. I wasn't sure why I expected her to call, not after the painful conversation we had. She accepted my departure with dignity and elegance, and that just made me want her more. She was a strong woman, the kind that didn't appear weak in front of anyone. She refused to let me hurt her, and that made me respect her. "No."

"Oh…that's too bad."

"Yeah." I drank my water, feeling the cool liquid moisten my dry throat.

"You haven't seen anyone in a while, then?"

Diesel wasn't around, so this conversation didn't feel so awkward. I felt like I could tell Titan things I couldn't say to my sons. Maybe it was because she was a woman. "No, not really. I was kinda seeing this woman from *Platform* magazine…but it didn't work out."

Her eyes narrowed on my face, and she cocked her head to the side. Nothing about what I said was particularly alarming, but the words obviously meant something to her. She leaned over the coffee table and picked up the very edition that had me slapped on the cover. "Scarlet Blackwood?"

I could only assume she'd read the article. "Yes."

"Vincent…she's really into you."

I read the article that was published, and while it was filled with flattery, I didn't think our romantic connection was obvious. "You're reading too much into it."

"No, I'm not." She set it down again. "I thought it when I read it, but now that I know you dated her…it's obvious."

My hands came together, the veins on the backs of my knuckles firm. Thinking about Scarlet bummed me out, but the idea of calling her filled me with guilt. No matter what I did, I was doomed.

"Why did you start seeing each other?"

I shrugged as I searched for an explanation. "It was too complicated."

"Complicated how?" she asked. "I've always heard Scarlet is a wonderful editor and an even more incredible person. You can judge someone's character based on what their employees think of them. And they have nothing but good things to say about her."

"Not surprising…"

Her eyes narrowed again, and this time, a smile accompanied it. "So you did like her?"

I knew I should shut up. "She's a lovely woman. Very poised, polite, interesting…"

"Then why don't you keep seeing her?"

I rubbed my fingers against the scruff along my jaw. I hadn't shaved in five days. The motivation to preserve my appearance had disappeared.

"She's in her forties, right?"

"Yeah…forty-two."

"So she's the first woman you've dated that's your own age."

"Not quite," I said with a chuckle. "I wish I was still in my forties."

"What did you guys do together?"

If I really wanted this conversation to halt, all I had to do was stop answering her questions. Or I could make an excuse and leave. Even just telling her that my personal life was none of her business would suffice. But I didn't want to do any of those things. I guess I wanted to keep talking about it. "We went to breakfast after I bumped into her one night. Then we went to the MET together before it opened…had dinner together. I enjoyed her company." I just enjoyed it a little too much.

"How long has this been going on for?"

"A few weeks," I answered. "We originally met so we could talk about the article, but our conversation went off on a lot of different tangents. Then we weren't talking about the article anymore, just having a real conversation. She has a daughter who's in nursing school right now. She was married once before, but apparently, it was a mistake. She has a great sense of humor…she's easy to talk to."

"I suspect she didn't call it off based on the article… so was it you?"

All I did was give her a nod.

"Why, Vincent? It sounds like you actually liked her." Titan's voice fell in intensity, and she was practically whispering. She must have sensed the delicate nature of the situation.

"I did like her," I admitted. "That was the problem…"

Softness touched her eyes, bringing a look of

sadness to the surface. "You've been with other women…"

"But they didn't mean anything to me. We were friends, of course. But it was just physical companionship. They were young women who enjoyed being spoiled by a rich man. I enjoyed the sex and so did they."

"So Scarlet is special to you?"

I nodded. "I feel my heart race when I'm near her. I feel my hands shake. I'm not just attracted to her appearance, but everything underneath the skin. I don't want to fuck her like the others. I want to make love to her. I haven't felt that way about anyone since…" It was too insulting to compare Scarlet to Isabella. I wouldn't dare say it out loud.

"Vincent…" She reached her hand for mine and held it. "I can't even imagine how that must feel."

"I hope neither of you loses each other so early in life." I squeezed her hand. "I never want my son to suffer the loss of the love of his life."

"I'm sure we won't. But if he did, I know I would want him to move on. I know I would want him to be happy."

I stared at our joined hands and understood what she was trying to say to me.

"She wouldn't want you to be alone, Vincent. I know I never met her, but I just know. You've waited long enough. You have so much life left to live. Don't waste the years you have left."

I pulled my hand away and straightened in my chair. "I never want to forget her…"

"You never will."

"I'm afraid if I let something happen with Scarlet, I'll be happy. And as my happiness grows, my memory of Isabella will fade. I won't think about her every day. I'll think about her less and less…and I don't want that to happen."

"You will think about her less, but that's okay. That doesn't mean you stopped loving her."

I promised to love that woman for the rest of my life. The second I laid eyes on her, I just knew. I never wanted to break the promise I made to her, not out of obligation, but because I meant that vow when I made it.

"What if your situations were reversed?"

I wished they were.

"Would you want her to move on, Vincent?"

"Depends."

"On?"

If Isabella had fallen in love with someone else, I wouldn't be upset about it. I would understand that she'd had to move on with her life. There would be no jealousy on my part. "I'd want her to be with a really great guy, someone who loved her as much as I did and would always take care of her. If he fit that criteria, I'd be happy."

"You don't think she'd feel the same way?"

I knew she would. "Yeah…"

"Then give this a chance, Vincent. You could be happy again."

Happiness was my biggest fear. The only glimpses of joy I received were from the nice moments with my family. Or when I explored the Mediterranean coastline with a beautiful woman by my side. Every moment was fleeting—and they didn't last long.

"Did you tell Scarlet why you left?"

I nodded. "She understands my circumstance. She's very compassionate."

"If she's willing to share your heart with Isabella, then she sounds like a wonderful woman."

"She is."

"I know I have no right to tell you what you should do. It's none of my business. But I don't think it's right that you keep punishing yourself. Loving another woman would never take away from how much you love your wife. If Scarlet understands that, then you have nothing to worry about. Just get her back before it's too late. If you wait too long, you never know what might happen."

I nodded in agreement, knowing she was right. Moving on was the hardest thing I'd ever had to do, and honestly, I never really had. I understood Isabella wasn't coming back, but I refused to share my life with someone new because I shared it with her ghost. I'd rather live with her memory than a real person. But I knew I couldn't do that forever. I shouldn't miss out on something that made me happy just so I could stay miserable.

Isabella would want me to be happy.

I knew that in my heart.

"You know Jax, Brett, and Diesel will be supportive. They want you to be happy."

"I know they do."

"Then do it, Vincent. And remember…" She extended her left hand, her diamond ring reflecting the light. I remembered exactly how it felt when I slipped that ring onto Isabella's hand. I remembered the night I gave it to her. Her face lit up with the brightest look of joy I'd ever seen. "None of us will ever forget her… because she's here with us now."

———

I waited outside Scarlet's building until she got off work. I considered calling her, but that wasn't personal enough for the situation. After the way I'd hurt her, I had to make up for it. I needed to do something that would be worthy of her forgiveness.

So I waited outside in the cold.

She stepped out shortly after five, dressed in heels and a long black jacket. Large shiny buttons were on the front, and her curled hair was pulled over one shoulder. Her sunglasses hung from the front of her jacket. Nothing about her seemed different. If she was still upset about our conversation, it didn't seem like it.

I stepped from the side and approached her from the right. I didn't want to startle her, so I said her name before I arrived. "Scarlet."

Her head snapped in my direction, and she couldn't control the reaction that contorted her face. She was shocked by my presence, probably because she assumed she would never see me again. "Vincent? Everything alright?"

"Yeah, everything is fine. I was hoping we could talk." Now that I was face-to-face with her, I didn't feel as confident as I usually did. I'd assumed she would still want me, but what if I was wrong? What if someone else had swept her off her feet? She was so beautiful that a guy in his early thirties would still want her.

"Uh…I guess." Flustered, she tucked her hair behind her ear. "I'm sorry, I'm just so surprised to see you here. I thought I would never see you again…unless it was in the papers or online or something."

"Can we go somewhere private? Maybe dinner?"

"Can't you just say whatever you need to say now?" She didn't retain the same calmness as she did before. Since I caught her off guard, she could only react emotionally. "I…I know that came out rude. It's just… I've been pretty upset since our last conversation, so if you have something to say about that, I'd rather hear it now. I can't wait until we're sitting in a restaurant. I need to know now. Because if you're here to tell me—"

"That I'm sorry and made a mistake?"

She immediately inhaled.

"That I've thought it over and have changed my mind?"

She exhaled.

"Yes, that's exactly what I wanted to say to you."

An emotional smile stretched across her face. "Then let's have that dinner."

———

The wine was poured and dinner was ordered. Now it was just us in a crowded restaurant, a flickering candle on the table between us. The lights were low, and it cast an exquisite glow across her face. After working all day, she still looked like she'd just finished fixing herself up. I loved the freckle on her cheek, the shade of her lipstick, and the thickness of her eyelashes.

I'd already stared a lot, but now I couldn't stop.

I should tell her how I felt. I should tell her what I did for the past week. I should tell her how conflicted I felt loving two women at the same time.

But I didn't say anything.

She didn't either. She swirled her wine before she took a drink. The lipstick smeared against the glass, and I remembered the way her kiss felt against my mouth. She must have thought of it too because she looked away, a little color in her cheeks. "How was your week?"

"My son is getting married next Saturday."

"Oh, that's exciting. Where?"

"Thailand."

"Oh wow, that's far…"

"But it'll be beautiful. And I wouldn't miss it for anything."

"That will be a lot of fun."

"Yeah, I'm sure it will." I wished my wife were there to witness it with me.

"I missed you." She held my gaze as the whisper left her lips. "I missed talking to you…I missed not talking to you."

I knew exactly what she meant. "Me too."

"I've gotten a lot of compliments on the article. But anytime someone mentioned it, I was only reminded of what I lost. Made it difficult to be proud of it."

"It's something to be proud of. I've never told anyone the things I told you."

"I know…people asked how I did it."

"And what did you say?" My fingers rested on the stem of my glass.

"I told them I understood you…and you understood me. It's the basis of all human connection."

It was a simple answer, but something so fundamental didn't need a complicated explanation.

"What made you change your mind?" She'd given me enough opportunities to start the conversation on my own. When I didn't cooperate, she gave me the push I needed.

"My future daughter-in-law."

Scarlet smiled. "What did she say?"

"She made me realize it was okay to move on, that

Isabella would want me to. I told Tatum you were the first woman that I've ever felt something for…that I've cared about. When I'm with you, I want to make love to you. I want to kiss you slowly even if it never goes anywhere. I want to see a movie on a Monday night because we can't find anything else to do. I want to show you the world as well as my sheets…but I also want more than that. It's more than companionship or friendship. It's…a lot more. With the other women I've been with, there was never anything substantial between us. But with us, I feel something. It reminds me of the way I felt for Isabella when I first started seeing her."

Her eyes softened. "That's really sweet, Vincent. I feel the same way."

"I've been living with my wife's ghost instead of living with a real person. I know she would want me to move on and be happy. I've never tried to move on before…until I met you. I just hope you can be patient with me…and understand that no matter what happens between us—"

"You'll always love your wife. I understand, Vincent." She gave me a smile. "I told you I didn't have a problem with that."

"Most women wouldn't be so understanding."

"And I probably wouldn't be either if I didn't like you so much. But they say there's no such thing as a perfect man. There's no such thing as a perfect woman. Love is about accepting each other for who they are. I understand your issues, and I have my own issues too.

But if we both look past those obstacles…I think we could find happiness."

That was exactly the reason I wanted Scarlet. She'd been understanding since the first time we met. Her affection for me grew as she got to know me. Her interest had nothing to do with my money or power. She had her own career that gave her joy. She didn't need me for anything. "That was well put."

She reached her hand across the table and opened her palm.

I eyed it for several seconds before I placed my hand on top. My callused fingers touched her soft ones, and I felt the same jolt of energy I felt when she kissed me. Her warmth mixed with mine, and I felt the friction between the tips of our fingertips. I watched our joined hands and felt a form of intimacy I never shared with Alessia or any of the others. It was the first time I really opened my heart, really accepted something new in my life. It was terrifying, still plagued with guilt, but it also felt wonderful.

Truly wonderful.

————

We got into the back seat of my car.

I eyed her hand on the leather seat beside me. Instead of thinking about every action before I made it, I moved my hand to hers and held it.

The corner of her mouth rose in a smile.

Touching a woman's hand wasn't difficult. Fucking them until they came twice wasn't hard either. I knew how to handle a woman. I knew how to handle several. But handling a woman who actually made my heart squeeze was a completely different story. Her touch meant so much more. "Would you like to come over?"

She turned my way in the car, the shadows casting different designs across her face. A smile was in her eyes, and slowly, it formed on her lips too. "I'd love to, Vincent. But there's no rush. We have plenty of time."

I didn't know what we would do once we got there, but I didn't want to say goodnight when I'd just gotten her back. She'd never seen my place, and I'd never seen hers. I'd asked her to as many public places as I could. I was running out of excuses to spend time with her. We could only eat so much. I turned to my driver. "Back to my place." I hit the button and raised the center divider.

We moved through the streets as we headed to my penthouse a few blocks away. Thankfully, my house-cleaners had just tidied up the place. I'd left my gas fire-place on, and the TV was still playing the game because I'd recorded it. When I had dates over, I usually offered them a glass of wine before we went to bed.

But they usually wanted to skip the wine.

I didn't know what I would do once I got Scarlet there.

I knew what I wanted to do.

But would that be the right thing to do?

Our hands remained locked together as my driver took us across town. Her legs poked out underneath her long jacket, and my eyes couldn't help but wander over her body. She had a beautiful figure. It was one of the first things I'd noticed.

After what seemed like a lifetime, the driver pulled up to my building.

Hand in hand, we walked inside and took the elevator to my floor. There were two properties on each floor, but I bought both just so I could have my privacy. No one could get access to this floor without the code, so it was impossible for anyone to get up there besides the fire marshal. With all the weirdos in the world, I didn't want them to follow me here.

I unlocked the door and we walked inside.

The second we were in my personal space, I felt the tension slowly sink down my spine. I'd never been more aware of the fact that I was alone with a woman. Scarlet and I were alone in that museum, but it wasn't the same.

Now there were four walls surrounding us—no interruptions.

"Can I take your coat?" I moved behind her and peeled the thick jacket off her shoulders.

"Sure." She stepped forward and took in the view of my penthouse. I had a large living room that was big enough for a dinner party for at least fifty people. A grand piano sat in the corner even though I never played. It was once owned by one of the greatest musicians of all time. It was a trophy as well as a piece of art. My couches were dark gray, and the rest of my furniture was decorated with dark cherry wood, black statues, and a comfortable rug. When I designed this property, I told the designer it would forever be a gentleman's space. I didn't go for a look that would fit into a Pottery Barn catalog. It was still sleek, elegant, and full of masculinity. Her gaze grazed over the scene in front of her, examining my large TV on the wall and the stone fireplace. "Your place is beautiful."

"Thank you. I can give you a tour later, if you'd like."

"How big is this place?"

"Twelve thousand square feet."

Her eyes snapped open, and then she released a restrained laugh. "Oh...Jesus." She laughed again, and this time, she covered her mouth. Her eyes still contained her laughter, but she slowly combated it. "Sorry...I wasn't prepared for that information."

It was a lot of space for one person. I didn't go into the other places in the house often. My personal gym was the only room I visited on a regular basis. The only reason why I kept the penthouse was because of the location. The views were spectacular, and it was close to work. "I've been here for about five years now." I walked to the bar against the wall, where I had everything I needed to entertain anyone—no matter their preference. "Would you like a drink?"

"Sure. I'll have whatever you're having."

I looked over my shoulder. "I'm having a scotch —neat."

She walked past my couch and grazed her hand over the material along the back. Her eyes took in everything, probably with the perception of someone who designed the layout of an entire magazine. "I like scotch."

"Really?" I turned back and made the drinks.

"Women can't like scotch, Vincent?" she asked playfully.

I joined her behind the couch and handed her the glass. "Of course not. I've only seen you drink wine."

"Because you always order a bottle for the table," she said. "But I do enjoy wine. I enjoy everything, actually." She brought the glass to her lips and took a small drink before she pressed her lips together. "That's smooth."

"That's the only way I take it." I took a drink with my eyes trained on hers. I concentrated my gaze on her prominent cheekbones, the pretty angles of her face. Her lips were plump and soft. My experience touching them was limited, but I'd never forget how they felt.

Once my attraction began to rise, I thought of my large mattress in my bedroom. With feather-soft sheets and a beautiful view of the city, it was the most romantic room in the penthouse. I could picture her underneath me, her legs spread as I slowly thrust into her. The collar of my shirt suddenly felt tight around my corded neck. A rush of heat erupted from my core and stretched to my extremities. My throat went dry, and my slacks suddenly felt tight when my cock thickened against my zipper.

Since I actually liked Scarlet, sex took on a different meaning. If I didn't care about her, sex wouldn't mean anything so I wouldn't put much thought into it. My hand would move into her hair, I'd kiss her, and then the clothes would come off.

But it was more complicated than that.

She watched me with her pretty green eyes, studying the stubble on my jaw as she continued to down her drink. "How about we make ourselves comfortable on the couch and watch the game? You recorded it?"

"Yeah…" She must have seen the red light on the DVR.

She took my hand and pulled me toward the couch. "I don't watch religiously, but I'm a fan." She sat down and crossed her legs with her drink still held in her hand.

I sat beside her, feeling the stress suddenly disappear from my shoulders.

She smiled at me then moved her hand to my thigh. Her hand was closer to my knee than my crotch, and I wondered if she did that on purpose because she noticed the bulge in my slacks.

I knew she took me into the living room on purpose. I knew she sensed my hesitation and understood I wasn't ready to move into the bedroom. Instead of pressuring me, she picked up on my emotions and made it easy on me. It was thoughtful. My hand moved to hers, nearly swallowing it up because my palm was so much bigger than hers. "It's not that I don't want you."

"I know, Vincent." She squeezed my hand then glanced at my crotch.

She definitely noticed it.

"There's no rush. It'll happen when it's meant to happen. I'm more than happy just to be with you, to enjoy this fine scotch in your beautiful home. I want a lasting relationship based on more than sex. I know I want you in a way I've never wanted another man, but I've waited this long for you…and I can wait a little longer."

My image was based on cold silence. I was known as a ruthless dictator of hundreds of corporations. I didn't show weakness, and I didn't express my feelings to anyone. To the world, I looked like a living slab of stone. Indifferent, cruel, and unforgiving, I brought a new definition to the word man.

It was nice to shed that skin. It was nice to show someone more. It was nice not to care about being strong all the time—because I certainly wasn't. "Thank you." My face was pressed closer to hers, and I could see the light from the TV reflect in her eyes. I loved the thickness of her eyelashes, the way her eyeliner made her eyes stand out more. I loved the way freckles sprinkled across her cheeks like small crystals of snow.

I leaned my face into hers automatically, and I found her lips. The second I felt her warmth, I sucked in a deep breath, making my lungs ache because they reached full capacity instantly. My lips felt hers, memorizing the way they felt against my mouth. My yacht excursions with Alessia were forgotten. Dinner in my chalet in Switzerland with Meredith faded away. Now I pictured the things I would do to this woman, the things I could give her. I wanted to take care of her, to deserve this kiss every single day.

It started off slow, just the way our last kiss did. But now there were no interruptions, and feelings were spilled onto the table. I wanted to kiss her just like this forever, to get to know her physically at a slow pace. The connection and excitement were there, so chemistry wasn't an issue.

Her hand moved to my shoulders, and her fingers dug into me. She sucked my upper lip before her kiss moved to the corner of my mouth. She had a sensual touch, full of confidence and longing. She breathed into me and kneaded me with her fingers. Sometimes a quiet moan would escape her lips, so quiet I wasn't sure if I heard it. She pulled on my jacket, getting me closer to her.

My hand moved to her knee and slowly slid up her thigh, feeling the soft skin along with the toned muscles underneath. My hand stopped before I ventured too far underneath her dress, but my fingers ached to reach a little farther. I wanted to touch her panties with my fingertips, to flick her nipples as they pebbled.

Our tongues came next, and then I was so hard it actually hurt.

I wanted to lay her on the couch and bury myself between her legs. It'd been months since Alessia. I used to get laid on a daily basis, wake up to a beautiful model riding me in the morning. Now I'd been in a drought because I was tired of the hollow sex.

I got more satisfaction out of a single kiss with Scarlet than I ever did with Alessia or the others.

It felt right.

And it didn't scare me as much as it used to.

## CHAPTER TEN

Diesel

Mrs. Diesel Hunt.

I liked it.

I liked it a lot.

In fact, I didn't want to wait to call her that. I wanted that privilege right here, right now. I didn't want to wait until our wedding in Thailand. I wanted to own this woman completely and irrevocably.

When I first started seeing Titan, it was a battle for dominance. She wanted to control me, and I wanted to control her. She was a fierce opponent, and I feared I would never win, I would only share power with her.

But now she yielded to me.

She was all mine.

There would be no fight. There would only be possession. She willingly submitted to me, not because I was stronger than her.

But because I earned it.

I rode the elevator to the penthouse I'd been sharing with her. We hadn't decided where we would live together because we were focused on the wedding—and the honeymoon. There were still a few other things we hadn't discussed it—like a prenup.

The doors opened, and I felt the testosterone spike in my blood. The entire time I was at the office, I was anxious to come back to her. Now I could act on every instinct I felt, I could take her in whatever way I wished. I would never have to let her overrule me again.

I was the king.

Even though I loved her, she was now my prisoner.

A willing one.

I stepped into the living room and found Thorn sitting beside her, paperwork spread out everywhere, two cups of coffee and their open laptops on the coffee table. Tatum was dressed for the office even though she hadn't returned to her building. Thorn was in a black suit with a black tie. Even though she was ready to return to work, Thorn was still handling most of her projects because he'd been running them for the past six weeks. She was leaving again for a long honeymoon, so it didn't make sense to pull Thorn off the job.

I had nothing against Thorn, but I didn't want to look at his face right now.

Tatum looked up when she saw me. "Hey, how was—"

"Thorn, Tatum will talk to you tomorrow." My eyes

remained glued to hers even though I wasn't speaking to her. I stripped my jacket off and tossed it on the floor.

Thorn didn't give me a smartass remark. He shoved everything into his satchel, the sound of moving paperwork filling the tense silence.

Tatum stared at me, her gaze darkening in irritation. "You're being a bit rude."

I undid my tie and pulled it out of my collar. I didn't toss it on the ground because I had other plans for it. "It's after five o'clock. Now it's my time."

Thorn shouldered the bag then walked to the elevator, the corner of his mouth raised in a slight smile. "I'll talk to you tomorrow, Titan."

"I apologize for Diesel's rudeness." She tossed her paper aside and crossed her legs.

Thorn stepped inside the elevator once the doors opened. "Don't worry, I get it." The doors shut and hid him from view.

I hadn't looked at him once, dismissing him as unimportant. I'd been at work all day while my woman stayed home. I'd warned her that things would be different, that I completely viewed her as my property now.

I unbuttoned the front of my shirt as I slowly approached her, my dress shoes slightly tapping against the hardwood floor. When I reached the rug, the movements were muffled, but my presence filled the space between us.

I stopped in front of her then placed the backs of

my fingers against the hollow of her throat. My eyes watched my movements, slowly sliding up along her neck until I reached her chin. I tilted her face up, forcing her to look at me.

My fingers slowly migrated into her hair, feeling the soft strands that held a gentle curl. My fingers invaded the strands, brushing her like a prized mare. I watched her breathing increase, witnessed the way she swallowed. The muscles of her throat shifted with the movement, telling me this encounter was making her hot under the collar.

I brushed my thumb across her bottom lip, as if I were a painter holding a brush. I felt her intricate features, exploring the prominent softness of her pale cheeks. As if she'd never been broken in her life, she looked absolutely perfect. Like a raw diamond that shone brighter than any jewel, she was the greatest prize in the known world.

And she was mine.

I wanted to wrap my fist around her entire body and squeeze. That ring on her finger wasn't a big enough declaration of my adoration. It wasn't strong enough to ward off the eyes that appreciated her body.

I wanted more of her. I didn't want to share her with anyone—especially the entire world.

I felt the silk tie between my fingertips, considering how I would use it. I could do anything I wanted to her, and the endless possibilities got me so hard I thought I might burst. I wrapped it around my knuckles before I stepped back. "Up."

Titan stared at me, her lipstick slightly smeared from the way my thumb brushed against it. There was a blooming fight in her eyes, her natural reaction to any order that was issued. But her resistance didn't last longer than an instant. She rose to her feet then faced me.

I didn't kiss her right when I walked in the door. There was no hug or embrace. The affection I wanted to give her was much different, much more intense. It might not be romantic, but I didn't give a damn if it was. "Turn around." I didn't raise my voice, but my command was heavy in just the tone. A real man didn't have to raise his voice in the first place.

Her lips parted slightly like she'd been expecting a kiss. She hid her disappointment and complied. As if she anticipated what I was going to ask, she placed her hands behind her back and waited for them to be bound.

I wrapped my tie around her wrists and secured them tighter than necessary. I wanted the silk to dig into her hands, for the pressure to remind her she was owned by one of the richest men in the world.

Me.

I checked the knot even though I knew it was tight. Then I guided her forward down the hallway and into the bedroom. I placed her at the foot of the bed before I undressed behind her, taking my time as I stared at her back. My collared shirt was tossed over the back of a chair, my slacks were kicked aside, and my shoes and socks were left on the floor beside me. I stripped down to my bare skin then pressed my hard chest against her back. My balls hit her hands as they held against her ass.

The second her fingers touched me, she slowly massaged my sac.

I locked my arms around her waist, and I pressed my mouth to her neck. I kissed her soft skin, giving her gentle kisses then aggressive nibbles. My tongue moved up her neck and I breathed in her ear, feeling her body soften and harden at the same time. Her fingers started to work me harder, and she turned her face into mine, practically begging for a kiss.

She wouldn't get a kiss until she earned it.

I teased her by brushing my mouth over hers, but I never let them connect. I could feel the metal ring she wore against my dick as she touched me, only reminding me that she belonged to me.

My hands gripped the fabric of her dress, and I slowly pulled it up, drawing it over her hips until it bunched around her waist. Her perky ass stuck out, the black thong contrasting against the fair color of her skin.

I hooked one finger inside her thong and slowly dragged it down, moving over her slender thighs until it was bunched around her knees.

Her back rose with the deep breaths she took, her

excitement obvious in her heavy breathing. Her dress was yanked up, and her panties were around her knees.

Perfect.

I grabbed the back of her neck and slowly pushed her to the bed, keeping the arch in her back as she moved. Her ass stuck out, and she placed her chin against the comforter. Her feet were still on the floor, but she pushed up on the balls of her feet.

I stood behind her with a twitching dick, admiring all the hills and valleys of this beautiful woman. I moved on top of her and pressed a kiss to the top of her spine. Her skin immediately pebbled with goose bumps as I migrated down her back, kissing the curve in her back then the top of her ass.

She tightened underneath me, her breathing becoming harsher. The anticipation was killing her, the purposeful wait that I was making her suffer. Her wrists stayed against her back, but she tested them time to time, as if she forgot the silk keeping her there.

My hands pressed against the mattress on either side of her hips, and I leaned into her, my heavy cock pressing into her ass. I started to grind against her, pushing against her luscious cheeks.

Her fingers reached for me, but I was too far away.

This woman was entirely mine to enjoy.

I grabbed her throat then tilted her head back as far as it would go. When her eyes reached mine, I tightened my hold on her neck. "Stay." I released her neck and pressed my hand against the mattress.

I pushed my dick into her soaked slit and sank deep. Both of my hands fisted the comforter underneath me as my cock absorbed her arousal like a sponge. There hadn't been an instance when I wasn't greeted by her slickness. She was always ready for me, at any time. I slid all the way inside, my size thickening and stretching her petiteness as wide as possible. I stared down at her face and watched the way she enjoyed it. When I pushed a little too far, her body immediately shifted. Sometimes I hit her cervix on accident because my length was too long.

For the first few seconds, I just enjoyed the way she felt. I memorized how her shoulders were pulled back because of the way her wrists were bound. The small muscles of her body were flexed and noticeable underneath the skin. She had been weak when she was recovering from her gunshot wound, but now she was back to her usual strength.

But she chose to bend for me.

I teased her with my cock, letting her feel how hard I was for her. I wanted to her feel the calm before the storm, to feel completely possessed by the man she gave her heart to. When I walked in that door, I wanted her all to myself. I didn't give a shit if Thorn was there. It could be the President of the United States, and I still wouldn't give a damn.

Without warning, I started to thrust hard. My weight drove her into the mattresses, and I pushed her deeper into the bed, making her shift up and down as I pounded into her hard. I hit her at the right angle, making her clit grind against the sheets underneath her.

She panted right away, her moans mingling with her heavy breathing. Her wrists writhed in their bindings as she tried to yank free. She didn't want to escape, but she wanted to turn around and touch me. I knew she wanted to drag her nails down my back and split me open.

But she didn't have the right to.

At this angle, I had her so deep. I had her so submissive. I already wanted to dump my load in her pussy. I wanted to do it over and over again. But my need for possessiveness restrained me.

She was about to come. I could feel it in the way she tightened around me. I could feel it in the way her breathing slowed.

I shoved myself completely inside her and remained still.

She growled in defiance.

I looked down at her face, seeing the redness in her cheeks and the hatefulness in her eyes. "Diesel…"

I ground against her, making her clit rub harder against the sheets underneath her.

She moaned as both of her hands formed fists.

"You. Are. Mine."

She hesitated before she answered, enjoying the friction I gave her. "Yes…"

"Yes, Boss Man."

Her breath came out shaky before she complied. "Yes, Boss Man."

I pulled out my dick then hooked my arm across her chest. I kissed her neck, slathering the skin with hot kisses and caresses with my tongue.

She writhed underneath me, enjoying it but also hating it. "Please…"

"Please, what?" I spoke into her ear.

"Please fuck me."

I kissed the corner of her mouth then rubbed my wet dick through the crack in her cheeks. "You want my cock, baby?"

"Yes, Boss Man…"

Watching my future wife beg for my dick was sexier than any threesome I'd ever had. I pushed down on the base of my dick and slid back inside her, greeted by her warmth and wetness.

"Yes…"

I thrust into her hard, picking up speed instantly. My dick already felt the spike of pleasure in my blood. He twitched in anticipation, knowing the impending orgasm would be as powerful as a tsunami. I thickened even further, the pressure inside her walls increasing. I hit my threshold but didn't let myself cross the finish line.

I wanted to tease her, not torture her.

I thrust and pressed her against the mattress at the same time, giving her everything she needed to push over the edge.

"God…" She was almost there. She was panting, writhing.

Then I stopped again.

"Diesel!"

I pressed my mouth to her ear. "Tell me you love me."

She breathed through the instant of silence, absorbing my words through her sex-crazed moment. Then she responded. "I love you, Diesel…"

I started to thrust. "Again."

"I love you."

I pounded into her harder, driving her into the end. "Again."

"God…" She started to come, squeezing my dick without mercy. "I love you…" Her fingers spasmed and her moans turned incoherent. Her hips bucked slightly, the pleasure reducing her to a quivering mess.

I hit my trigger when I heard those words fall out of her mouth. My cock gave a final twitch, and I emptied deep inside her, filling her pussy with my enormous load. I'd fucked her before I went to work, but that was over eight hours ago. That was pretty much a different day.

I felt my own come surround me as I filled the minimal space she had. My fingers dug into the sheets, and I steadied my breathing, feeling the goodness sweep over me as the pleasure radiated from my core to every extremity. I loved to control this woman, to dominate her in a way no one else ever had. I got to do it for the rest of my life, to own her.

To make her a Hunt.

I pulled on the tie and undid the knot with two fingers.

Her wrists were marked from the constriction, and her hands came apart slowly, the muscles in her shoulders tense from staying that way for so long. She lay flat for a moment, recovering from the exertion as well as the pleasure.

I kept my dick inside her and kissed the back of her neck, my chest rubbing against her slender back. Her diamond ring still sparkled in the limited light, reminding me that she was always mine. I kissed her shoulders and spine next, treasuring her after the harsh way I took her like a piece of property.

She was my property.

Just as much as I was her property.

I slowly pulled out of her, my softening cock still slick from her arousal. My come was smeared across her stretched slit, and I enjoyed the view. I was a man, and like all men, I was proud of what I'd just done. "I'm gonna take a shower." I kissed the back of her shoulder.

She rose on her arms and slowly moved off the bed, looking like the sexiest thing in the world with her panties around her knees and her wrists marked from the binding of my tie. Come dripped down the center of her thighs. "I'm going to join you."

"No." I stood in front of her and moved my hand

into her hair. I gripped her and directed her stare on my face. "You're keeping that come inside you until I'm ready to fuck you again. So pull your thong on and wait for me."

Her eyes flashed at the way I spoke to her, but she didn't dare deny me.

I released her hair and turned away. "Hope you're looking forward to being Mrs. Hunt as much as I am." I moved to the door, not expecting an answer.

Her voice reached me just before I stepped out. "I am."

———

I stepped inside Illuminance and immediately received looks from the staff in the lobby. They knew exactly who I was and my future stake in the company—in all the companies Tatum owned. The women stared at me the hardest, not flashing a single smile my way. Their looks were hollow and blank, like they were witnessing a legend they'd only heard rumors about.

The elevator took me to the top floor, where Tatum's office was held, along with the important personnel she liked to keep close. It was her first official day back at work, and she had walked out of the penthouse in a new pair of stilettos and an elegant outfit.

She looked sexy as hell.

My woman was back in the game. Her attacker was lying in a grave somewhere, but she was still running the world like the powerhouse she was. A bullet wasn't strong enough to take her down because she was invincible.

I walked up to Jessica's desk, one of the four assistants who ran most of Tatum's schedule.

When she saw me, she immediately rose to her feet. "Mr. Hunt, Titan isn't in her office right now. She's in a meeting with Ms. Alexander and Mrs. Cutler. She told me if you ever come by, I should take you to wherever she is."

I couldn't suppress the smile that spread across my face. I'd never had that kind of privilege before, even when we were officially seeing each other. Like everyone else, I had to check in and wait until she was ready for me. But now I had a special pass that allowed me to go anywhere and do anything I chose.

"I'll take you to the conference room."

"I know the way." I walked away from her desk and entered the large hallway. There were a few conference rooms on the floor, but there was only she would use. It had a great view of the city, and despite the glass doors, it contained privacy.

I approached the room and saw the three of them sitting together, their laptops in front of them along with notebooks and pens. Tatum looked stunning in the black blouse she wore with golden buttons down the front. Her hair was pulled back loosely, some soft strands coming free. With dark eye shadow and painted lips, she looked ready for the runway rather than a meeting.

Thorn was in a black suit with a pink tie. Concentrated and focused, he didn't seem to pay special attention to Ms. Alexander. Tatum told me they were sleeping together, and I couldn't hold it against him because I wasn't any better.

I'd fucked Tatum the first chance I got.

I stepped inside and watched them all turn to me.

Ms. Alexander gave me a professional smile along with a slight nod.

Thorn saluted me. "Diesel, you're right on time. We're breaking for lunch soon."

I walked around the table and shook his hand as I went. Thorn had been nothing but pleasant to me since my name had been cleared. Now he went out of his way to be friendly toward me, to make up for the harsh things he said to me.

I wasn't the kind of man to hold a grudge. He was Tatum's family, so now he was my family. "Good. I should make Tatum eat."

"Good luck with that," Thorn said with a chuckle. "That's like getting a goat to dance."

"Are you comparing me to a goat?" Tatum's eyebrow was cocked so high on her face it was about to jump off.

"What?" Thorn asked. "Goats are cute."

"They're farm animals," she snapped. "I'm not a farm animal."

Tatum was at the head of the table, so I came around until I reached her chair. I pushed one hand against the table and leaned down to kiss her.

That shut her up.

I kept the kiss PG, but it was still inappropriate for a business meeting. But whether she was meeting Thorn or a room full of suits, I didn't care. My presence only strengthened hers. She was a powerful woman with incredible wealth, but with a husband like me, she was truly untouchable. If they fucked with her, they fucked with me.

And believe me, you didn't want to fuck with me.

When I pulled away, I saw the affection in her eyes. The rest of her face was a professional mask, but that was one aspect she couldn't hide—at least, from me. She reacted to my touch no matter how many pairs of eyes stared at her. She was mine, and she knew I would claim her in front of anyone. "How's it going?"

"Good." Tatum tucked a loose strand behind her ear, acting innocent despite the way I fucked her when I came home yesterday. "We were just working on the first product line we're releasing as a company. We're attending the trade show in Chicago this weekend."

"The week before our wedding?" I asked incredulously.

Tatum shrugged. "I'm taking two weeks off for the honeymoon, so it's now or never. It'll be a great opportunity to showcase it, get people talking about it, have our PR team publicize it, and build up buzz before we drop it next month." She was back to business as usual, juggling a million things at once. As if she'd never been shot at all, she was back to full capacity.

"I'm coming along." I took a seat in the chair to the right of her, getting in position between her and Thorn. I wasn't part of this project and didn't know a lot of details, but I knew enough. "When are we leaving?"

Tatum didn't make an argument. "Friday night. We'll take my jet."

"Alright."

Tatum gave me a look before she turned away. She probably wanted to tell me to stay in Manhattan to catch up on all the work I missed out on, but she wouldn't say anything in front of her partners.

She turned back to her computer and addressed Ms. Alexander. "Do you think there are any improvements to be made? What is the likelihood someone else can reproduce this?"

Ms. Alexander was a lot more professional than I was even though she was sitting across from Thorn. "There will always be someone out there who can copy it. They can dissect my work and figure it out. But by then, there will be a new and better line out. It's the same thing with iPhones. By the time the competition catches up, a new one is out."

I glanced at Thorn and saw him stare so hard at Ms. Alexander that he looked pissed.

"Any chance of a patent?" Titan asked.

"On certain aspects, yes," Ms. Alexander said. "But

not everything can be protected. That's just how it goes."

They spoke for a few more minutes, tying up their meetings so they could break for lunch. When they were finally finished, they left their laptops and notes on the table.

"What are you guys in the mood for?" Tatum asked.

I knew what I was in the mood for.

"Salad," Ms. Alexander said.

"Me too," Thorn said. But he probably would agree with anything Ms. Alexander said.

"Is that alright with you, Diesel?" Tatum turned to me, doing her best to regard me with indifference.

She failed miserably. "Anything you want, baby."

We went across the street to a café and sat at a small table against the window. We immediately got service and ordered our drinks and lunches before we were left to our own conversation.

My hand rested on Tatum's slender thigh, my fingers digging into the fabric that covered her skin. I wanted to pull it up a bit and touch her bare skin, but I also didn't want any of the men to stare at her.

Even though they were already staring.

It didn't feel like just Tatum and I were together, but it felt like we were on a double date. It was not public information that Thorn and Ms. Alexander were hooking up off the clock. It wasn't my business to know that, but of course, Tatum told me. She was angry in the beginning but quickly got over it. She said she thought there could be more between Thorn and Ms. Alexander than good sex.

That Thorn might actually like this woman.

Thorn didn't look at her once as he sat beside her on their side of the table. He didn't make small talk with her either. His deliberate indifference only made their connection stronger. I could feel it in the air around us.

Ms. Alexander didn't look at him either, choosing to stare out the window or look at Tatum. Her legs were crossed and so were her arms. She possessed the same poise Tatum did, and she also dressed in the same elegant way.

I suspected the two of them would be close friends very soon.

"Are you going to see your parents while you're in Chicago?" Tatum broke the silence with a simple question.

"I have to," Thorn said. "My mom will scratch my eyes out if I don't stop by."

Ms. Alexander smiled, her eyes shining slightly.

Thorn still didn't look at her. "If she found out I went to Chicago and didn't tell her...I'd get death threats."

Tatum rolled her eyes. "She would not give you death threats. She's sweet as pie."

"Oh, she's sweet, alright," Thorn said. "But not when you cross her. And when her eldest son doesn't stop by, there's hell to pay. One time I was in Chicago for a single night before I flew back to Manhattan, and somehow, she figured it out." He shook his head. "The phone call I got the next day...terrifying. She doesn't cry and make me feel guilty. She screams at me like a sergeant in the military."

Tatum chuckled. "I still can't picture it..."

"Because she likes you," Thorn said. "She doesn't always like me."

My hand moved Tatum's dress up slightly, enjoying the soft skin of her thigh. "Ms. Alexander, are your parents like that?"

"No," she said with a chuckle. "But they live close by."

"Connecticut is a bit of a commute," Thorn said. "About an hour."

I cocked an eyebrow, interested that Thorn knew anything about her parents.

Tatum wore the same expression.

Ms. Alexander seemed slightly unnerved by his statement. "Yeah, but they're just a train away. I talk to my mom regularly. They've never really been clingy or overly affectionate. But if they lived in Chicago, they'd probably feel the same way."

"Are you an only child?" I asked.

"Yep," Ms. Alexander said. "So our family's legacy and reproduction have fallen to me...unfortunately."

"But you want to have kids," Thorn said. "It's not like it's a burden."

This time, Ms. Alexander flashed him a glare, silencing him with her ferocity.

Thorn looked away.

Now it was awkward again. Ms. Alexander obviously wanted to keep things professional, but Thorn didn't want to keep up a charade now that he'd told Tatum everything about his personal life. The production they were putting on really had no meaning.

Thorn turned back to her. "They know we're sleeping together. So let's just be real."

Ms. Alexander took a deep breath, but her eyes turned into daggers. "That's our personal life. I don't see why we need to talk about it…especially right in front of them."

"They're my family, baby," Thorn whispered. "I respect your desire to remain professional, but these are the people I see all the time. They know everything about my life. It just seems pointless…"

Ms. Alexander looked away, dismissing the conversation.

"He's right," Tatum said. "We're all friends here. I don't think there's any need to put up a fake image when we're all involved. We all have the maturity not to let it interfere with work." She gave Ms. Alexander a smile. "So, relax."

"See?" Thorn moved his hand to her thigh under the table.

She didn't push it away.

I couldn't gauge their relationship by watching them. In public, their feelings weren't so obvious. But judging by the way Thorn wanted to be open about what they had, their relationship did seem different from all the others.

I never put my hand on a woman's thigh in a restaurant.

Except the one woman I wanted to marry.

"Diesel." Thorn turned to me. "When's the bachelor party?"

I was way too fucking old for a bachelor party. "Never."

"Never?" Thorn asked incredulously. "You only get married once."

"Yes, I'm looking forward to it." I didn't want to slip a bill into a stripper's thong. I didn't want to smoke cigars with men in the middle of a strip joint to relive my days as a single man. I didn't want to get stupid drunk with a woman under each arm. Those days were long over. "I'm thirty-five. I don't need a bachelor party."

"Who cares how old you are?" Thorn countered. "We should celebrate."

"I'm good," I said dismissively.

"Please tell me you aren't going to be lame." Thorn turned to Tatum next.

She smiled. "Very lame."

Thorn rolled his eyes. "When did the richest couple in the world become the lamest couple? Diesel, you're supposed to watch women get naked one more time.

And Tatum, you're supposed to dance on a stage with a guy wearing nothing by a thong."

Tatum grimaced. "Honestly, that doesn't sound fun at all."

"And why would I want to watch women get naked? I've got the hottest woman in the world right here." I leaned into Tatum and kissed her on the cheek.

Thorn rolled his eyes again. "Fine. Say goodbye to your youth in the most pathetic way possible."

"I've seen it all," I said. "I've done it all. I said goodbye to that life the second I met Tatum. It's not like I'm getting married young and missing out on anything. I've lived a life of single misery for too long."

Ms. Alexander's eyes softened.

Thorn's did too, but he did a better job of hiding it.

"And if Tatum really wants to go out and watch a guy dance in a thong, she can watch me." I turned to her. "Isn't that right, baby?"

She chuckled. "I can't picture you doing that."

"But I'm sure you can picture me doing other things." My hand moved farther up her thigh, taking the dress with it. "I'll be your bachelorette party. And you be my bachelor party. We'll get stupid drunk. We'll get naked. And we'll do crazy shit that we won't remember."

"Now, *that* sounds like fun," Ms. Alexander said.

"Well…" Thorn inched closer to her. "If you're looking for a stripper, I'm available."

She grinned then pushed him away. "Good thing I'm not looking."

"Oh, come on." He circled his arm around her shoulders. "I dance as well as I—"

"Professionalism from this point onward." She pushed his arm down. "I mean it, Thorn."

Thorn sighed and turned back to us, but he didn't unleash a smartass comment like he usually would. She had some invisible power over him, a power I could see but perhaps he couldn't. They did have an obvious chemistry, and Thorn was playful with her in a way I'd never seen him behave toward anyone else.

Tatum was right…there was something more there.

## CHAPTER ELEVEN

THORN

*Come over.* I stared at my phone and waited for an answer.

*No.*

*Baby.*

*Don't call me that.*

*Sexy baby.*

The three dots didn't appear.

*Then I'll come to you.*

*I won't answer the door.*

This conversation wasn't productive, so I called her. I held the phone to my ear and listened to it ring. No answer. I hung up and texted her. *We're having this conversation. You don't get a choice.*

*You bet your ass, I get a choice.*

*Alright. I'm heading over.* I stayed on the couch because I knew she wouldn't call my bluff.

My phone started to ring.

I grinned then answered. "Sexy baby."

"Don't call me that either."

"Why? I like it. It's perfect for you."

"Well, I don't like it."

"Bullshit. You want to listen to me call you that while I come inside you." Now I was calling her bluff. I knew exactly how she reacted to me, to every touch, to every look.

She didn't argue. "I'm disappointed in you right now."

"Why?"

"Don't *why* me," she snapped. "You promised to stay professional."

"I *am* being professional. If I weren't, I would fuck you on the table in front of Titan."

"I'm being serious, Thorn. You told her about us, and now I feel like she views me as some slut."

I shook my head. "I promise you she doesn't think that."

"You don't know…"

"No, I do know. Titan would never, ever call another woman that. She's a hardcore feminist and thinks it's bullshit that men can sleep around and it's almost desirable. If a woman wants a physical relationship with a man, she lacks morals and she's a whore… she despises that. The only way we're going to change that is if all of us stop throwing those degrading terms around. So, no, she doesn't think that."

Autumn was silent.

"Trust me, it doesn't affect her opinion of you. She admires your brains and your success. All she cares about is the work, nothing else. Alright?"

She sighed into the phone. "You still told me we would remain professional."

"That's as professional as I can be. I'm not staying on this project forever. When Titan comes back from her honeymoon, I'll catch her up, and then I'll be gone. You won't have to work with me ever again. It'll be alright."

She turned quiet again.

"Now…are you coming over here, or am I going over there."

She scoffed into the phone. "Right to the point, huh?"

"Are you saying you don't want me tonight?"

Silence.

"That's what I thought. So, what's going to be?"

She stayed on the phone, considering her answer. Then she said, "I have to be up early tomorrow for my spin class."

"Then I'll go over there. See you in a bit, sexy baby."

————

The clothes were gone the second I stepped inside her townhouse. I sat in the center of her sofa with the bottoms of my feet pressed against the floor. I pushed against the ground to lift my hips upward, to meet her thrusts. I rested against the cushioned back of the couch, her tits in my face and my hands on her hips.

Fuck.

Me.

I slipped a beautiful pink nipple into my mouth and felt her pussy spasm around my dick as she came for the second time. She rode me harder, getting herself off with my huge dick wedged deep inside her. Her nails started at my shoulders then pulled all the way down, scratching into the sweat and skin. "Thorn…god." Her head rolled back, and she ran her hand through her hair.

Jesus.

I gripped her ass cheeks and squeezed them hard, feeling my dick start to beg. He was swallowed in her tight goodness, in a place more beautiful than anywhere else he'd been. Every time I moved inside her, my resistance waned. My fingers dug into her harder to hold on, but I was slipping.

My hand anchored in her hair, and I pulled her down on my crotch, shoving my dick far inside her. I released with a grunt, filling her pussy with so much come it pushed past my cock and smeared to my base, mixed with her own cream. I gripped her tits and rested my neck against the back of the couch, letting the orgasm stretch on until it slowly faded away.

She still rode me, her movements slowing down as

my cock began to soften. She was stuffed with come and cream, her pussy my favorite place in the world. Her arms wrapped around my neck, and she rested against me, her face just inches from mine.

"Sexy baby…" I kissed her top lip, tasting the sweat that formed there. I was sweaty too, but she was the one who did all the work. I just got to sit there and enjoy. "You love that name, right?"

"Only when I'm full of you."

I smiled against her mouth before I kissed her again. "You have the most incredible pussy…"

She smiled back. "I know."

"You know?" I asked with a chuckle.

"Well, your dick already told me that."

"Yeah…he makes it pretty obvious." My fingertips fell down her shoulder blades and her back, slowly moving down to her ass. I lightly caressed her everywhere, feeling the soft skin mixed with sweat. She had the most beautiful figure, an hourglass shape with phenomenal tits.

She leaned back slightly, still full of my softening cock. "I think I'm going to shower."

"Nope." I stood up and lifted her with me, keeping my cock inside her as I carried her into the hallway. I hadn't been in her bedroom yet, and I walked into the first room I saw. It was feminine, with lots of light colors and fluffy pillows. I set her on the bed then moved underneath the covers. "Wow, your bed is comfy."

"That's why I only lie in it when I'm going to

sleep…otherwise, I'll never get anything done." She pulled the covers back and got comfortable beside me, her makeup smeared slightly and her hair a mess.

I thought she'd never looked hotter. "I'm sleeping here tonight."

"Really?" she asked. "I thought we didn't do that."

"Well, now we do." My arms cradled her smooth body, and I pulled her tighter against me. We were both warm and sweaty, but I wanted her right beside me. I'd spent the day keeping my hands to myself, and now that we were alone together, I wanted to be all over her—all the time. "Don't pretend that you want me to leave."

When she didn't answer, I assumed it was a silent admission. "What exactly did you tell Titan?"

"About us?"

"Yeah." She watched me through her thick lashes, her eyes glowing with their own light.

"The truth."

"But how much of the truth?"

Her eyes narrowed. "Tell me what you said."

"Pretty much everything."

Her eyes narrowed further. "Everything?"

"You have to remember…she's my best friend. Shit, she's my *only* friend. I had to tell her about you because I told you the truth about my relationship with her. So she wanted to know the extent of ours…so I told her."

"And what did she say about it?"

"Nothing really…" I considered telling her what Titan really said. I wanted to pursue Autumn in a

different way, but I wasn't even sure where to begin.
How would she feel about it? "I told her I cared about
you…that you're the only woman I'm seeing. So she got
her hopes up and said she wants it to turn into something more."

"Really?" she whispered.

"Yeah, she wants me to settle down. She made a
fool out of me to the entire world, so it would make her
happy if I was happy."

"Well…are you happy?" Her gaze was locked on to
mine, watching every single shift of my eyes.

"That's actually something I wanted to mention
to you…"

"I'm listening."

"Titan and I had an arrangement because it suited
both of us. I'd be a great husband and father. She'd be a
great mother and wife. We both have considerable
wealth that would make us unstoppable together. It was
a perfect match. Not to mention, we trusted each other
implicitly. It took away the issues of heartbreak and
disappointment. Now she's fallen in love, and she
prefers a romance based on passion and longing…two
things that might disappear over time. She understands
that, but she's willing to risk it."

Autumn didn't let a single expression escape on her
face. She watched me calmly, listening instead of
jumping to conclusions right away.

"I already told you I don't see myself feeling something deep for another person, so I'm still open to this

idea. I want a family. I've always wanted to be a father. But the pressure of being in a romantic relationship is just too much. I'm an honest guy, so I'd always treat my wife with respect, take care of her, and be there for her. I'd never lie to her. With me, she'd have a man who treated her like a goddess. I'm sure I would love her… just never fall in love with her. I'd be with other women, but that wouldn't be a secret. They'd have my bed, but they wouldn't have my loyalty, not like she would. We'd raise a beautiful family and love our kids together. It'd be a partnership. You mentioned your hesitance to another relationship. Is this something you would consider?"

Instead of blurting out an answer right away, she didn't say anything at all. At least she wasn't repulsed by the idea. Most people wouldn't understand it and would just think there was something wrong with me. But at least she gave it some thought. "Are you asking me to be your wife…?"

Was that a yes? "I'm asking if you're open to the idea."

She turned quiet again, thinking about it in silence. "In this scenario, you would have relationships with other women?"

"Not relationships. Just flings. But, yes. It wouldn't be a secret. I wouldn't parade that in front of our family or anyone else. It would be a secret to everyone else besides the two of us."

That was the moment her eyes fell. She looked at the sheets between us, no longer holding my gaze.

I felt the disappointment inside me grow, knowing her answer before she actually gave it.

"I couldn't do that part. I could do everything else…but that."

"You'd have your own relationships too. It's a two-way street."

"I know I wouldn't want a relationship…" She slipped out of the bed and ran her fingers through her hair. "I'll be back…I'm going to shower." She crossed the room, her womanly hips swaying as she walked. Her black hair trailed down her back and shifted as she moved. She stepped into the bathroom then lightly shut the door behind her.

I propped myself up and stared at the closed door, trying to decipher what her last statement meant. She didn't seem horrified by my proposition until the end of my explanation. One moment, she was cuddled in my arms. And in the next instant, she was gone.

Now I was in bed by myself—and I'd never felt more alone in my life.

———

Titan and I sat across from each other in her office, going over the new product line for her Illuminance brand. We did beta testing in Budapest, but her products didn't leave the shelves. We weren't sure if it was the branding, price point, or the market.

Fortunately, my business was straightforward. It was machine-operated, and people needed canned tomatoes for everything. Food never went out of style, so I was always safe. Marketing in the food space was the opposite of what Titan was doing. Preserving old labels made the product seem more antique, and that's what people preferred in my realm. For everything else, like makeup and technology, it had to seem as modern and sleek as possible.

Autumn wouldn't be joining us that afternoon because she was busy in her lab. She only met with us when we discussed numbers and branding. The rest of the time, she was concentrating on creating or improving new products.

Titan's phone lit up so she glanced at it. "I should get going. I have to pick up the dress from Chase."

"Can't you send someone to do that for you?"

"You think I'm gonna let anyone touch my dress?" she asked incredulously. "I wouldn't even let Diesel touch it."

I stared at my paper and scribbled another note. My mind wasn't in the game that afternoon because I kept thinking about Autumn. When I'd left the next morning, she was just as quiet and timid as she was the night before. When I asked her about it, she said she was fine.

I knew she was lying, but I couldn't get her to tell the truth if she refused to share it with me.

"Thorn?"

"What?" I blurted without looking up.

"Did you hear what I said?"

"Yeah, you need to pick up your dress." I clicked the back of the pen so the tip disappeared.

"No. After that."

Shit, I must have missed it. "Uh, what?" I looked up, meeting her penetrating gaze.

"Everything alright? You've been weird all day."

"Didn't sleep well last night. That's all."

Titan saw right through that. "You drag everything out of me, so you know I'm gonna drag everything out of you."

I spun the pen in my fingertips, fidgeting even though I wasn't the kind of man to fidget. "I mentioned a convenient marriage to Autumn, and she seemed open to the idea in the beginning...but then she brushed me off."

"Just because we understand the perks of it doesn't mean other people will."

"I understand. But she didn't hate the idea in the beginning. When I told her we didn't have to be monogamous, that's when I lost her. She said she wouldn't want another relationship...then she walked off into the shower."

"Hmm...sounds like she's looking for a real partner, then."

"Maybe." I stared at my pen.

"Are you alright?"

"Yeah…I guess I'm just disappointed. If she said yes, that would be perfect."

"Perfect because?" She propped her chin on her knuckles.

"Because Autumn is perfect. I'd have a trophy wife who's also a genius. Come on, what could be more perfect than that?"

She leaned back into her white leather chair and crossed her arms. "Thorn, why don't you just do the actual marriage thing?"

"Because I don't want to. You know this."

"But you obviously like Autumn a lot. Maybe see where it goes."

I shook my head. "You know I'm not the committed type. Her last man left her for someone else. I'd kill myself if I ever hurt her. I never want to cause her pain. She's a good person and doesn't deserve that."

A slow smile formed on her lips. "You've got it bad."

"Just because I respect the woman doesn't mean I've got it bad."

"If you respect her, then yes. You're really into her. Come on, Thorn. When have you ever respected anyone?"

"Uh, you?" I said like a smartass.

"And we're best friends," she said slowly. "We've been together for over a decade now. You love me, and I love you. Now this woman has come into your life, and you feel close to her too…but you're attracted to her. Do I need to spell it out for you?"

I had stopped fidgeting with my pen, but now I started up again. "I'm glad you've fallen head over heels for Diesel, but that doesn't happen to everyone."

"True. But you need to stop dismissing the idea completely. Keep an open mind."

I dropped the pen into the inside pocket of my jacket. "People don't change."

"Some do. I know I have."

I rose to my feet and came around the desk. "Don't you have somewhere to be?"

She didn't move. "Thorn, as your friend, it's my job to tell you what you don't want to hear."

"Well, stop being my friend for two seconds."

She sighed then left the chair. She grabbed her purse off the table and pulled it over her shoulder. "Let me put this into terms you'll understand." She moved to the front of the desk, facing me on the other side. "If you don't make this work, some other guy will come into the picture and make it work. She'll move on and forget about you, and you'll sit around thinking about the woman you can't have. Now, is that a fate you're willing to accept? Is that a chance you're willing to take?" She stared me down, watching every single expression I made like a scientist studying something under the microscope.

I clenched my jaw and held her gaze, but I felt the tightness in my back and shoulders. I could lie to myself and say I wasn't jealous when other men looked at Autumn. I could pretend she didn't mean anything to me when we both knew she did. But the idea of moving forward terrified me.

Because I didn't want to hurt Autumn.

---

I didn't get much done during the first twenty minutes because I kept thinking about what Titan had said about Autumn. It circled in my mind over and over again. Was Titan right? Or was I right? Finally, I started to focus again and get stuff done.

Then Jessica shattered my concentration. "Sir, I have a Bridget Creed here to see Titan."

My blood stopped circulating in my body because it froze. I'd never forget that name because of the implications of her relationship to Titan. Diesel told me the truth, and I knew exactly who she was.

In light of everything going on in our lives, I'd forgotten about her altogether.

But now the hair on the back of my neck stood on end.

She was here to see Titan—again. What did she want this time? "Send her in, Jessica." I could send Bridget away and say Titan was out for the afternoon, but that sounded like a recipe for disaster.

I wanted to know what this woman wanted.

And I wanted to make sure she knew she couldn't fuck with Titan.

Bridget walked in a moment later, wearing a black dress with pearls around her neck. Her brown hair was pinned back in an elegant updo. Her nails were perfectly manicured, and she didn't look like a woman who needed money. She had such a startling resemblance to Titan that it baffled me the media hadn't seized upon this information. She didn't hide her disappointment when she saw me instead of Titan. "Mr. Cutler?"

"Hello, Mrs. Creed. How can I help you?" I rose to my feet and slid my hands into my pockets. I didn't want to seem threatening because this woman didn't appear to be dangerous, but I couldn't lower my guard. Since her motives were hidden from me, it was extremely unnerving. If I knew what she wanted, sinister or not, I'd be able to understand her.

But I didn't understand her at all.

She slowly walked farther into the room, a large wedding ring on her finger. The diamond was big and clear, an expensive piece of jewelry. Judging by the ring and the nice clothes she wore, she didn't seem like someone who needed money. But then again, maybe she'd had it but pissed it all away. "I came by to speak to Titan. Is she available?"

I held her gaze without blinking, confused by the innocence in her features. Last time, she seemed genuinely concerned about Titan. But now that she was there again, it seemed like she wanted something else. "No."

She stopped behind the two chairs that faced the desk, keeping the furniture between us.

"As you know, she's well again. Otherwise, you wouldn't be standing inside this office right now."

She didn't deny it, keeping her green eyes on me. Her features were so similar to Titan's that I felt like I was looking at my friend in a time machine. "If she's well again, why hasn't she returned?"

"She has. She had an appointment this afternoon." I kept the desk between us instead of walking around to shake her hand. Without understanding her purpose, I wouldn't show her any politeness. "But I suggest you stop dropping by like this. You have no purpose here."

Her eyes narrowed just the way Titan's did.

"Yes, I know who you are."

She inhaled sharply, taking my words like a knife to the heart. She looked away, her eyes instantly moist. Her strong posture immediately slouched, and her shoulders rolled forward. Like a boulder had landed on top of her, she seemed to be pushed toward the earth. "You do?"

"I suspected it the first time I looked at you. Same eyes…same hair…same everything."

"That's not enough evidence."

"No. But a PI is."

She dropped her gaze. "Does she know…?"

Should I divulge that information? I could lie and say Titan didn't want to see her, but that felt morally wrong. Titan said she wanted nothing to do with her, but if she were face-to-face with her mother, she might change her mind. "No."

"Why haven't told you her?"

"We told her we think you're her mother, but Titan said she didn't care whether you were or not. It doesn't make a difference to her."

She took another deep breath, the features on her face tightening from the blow. "Of course she hates me...how could I expect her not to?" As if she was feeling off-balance, she moved to the chair facing the desk and lowered herself onto the cushion. Her chin dipped to the floor in weakness, and her hands came together for strength.

I didn't lower myself into the chair, choosing to stand over her. I watched every movement she made and tried to understand if this display was sincere.

"I thought if I told her in person...maybe she would have some compassion."

"She doesn't hate you, Bridget."

She slowly looked up and met my gaze. Her eyes were wet, but the tears didn't form. "She doesn't...?"

"No. She understands you had to abandon her because you weren't ready to be a mom. Since you didn't want to stay, she thinks it's better that you walked away. You would have done her a disservice by forcing yourself to do something you didn't want to do. So, she doesn't hate you. But since you did abandon her, she doesn't want you in her life either. You made your choice, and you have to stick with it. You can't have it both ways."

"I...I understand why she feels that way. She's such a brilliant woman...so logical."

I finally lowered myself into the chair and watched her.

"I know she doesn't need me. I know she doesn't need anyone. But when I saw the news..." She gripped her chest, and that's when the tears started to well up. "I've never felt so scared in my life. I've never been so angry. Knowing your child is suffering...is the worst feeling in the world."

"But she's not your child, Bridget. You gave up that right twenty-five years ago."

She wiped her tears away with her fingertips. "Maybe...but I'll always see her as my daughter."

"When did you realize who she was?"

"Years ago. She did an interview with a fashion magazine. I saw her on the cover...and I knew."

"So you know she's the richest woman in the world?"

Her eyes burned with hostility. "Yes. But I don't want her money, Mr. Cutler. I guess I have to make that clear..."

"It's an odd coincidence," I said coldly. "She almost dies, and you wonder if you're the next of kin..."

Her eyes narrowed further. "I don't expect you to believe me, but no, that's not why I came into this office. A smart woman like her prepared for her death the second she had money. I'm sure she put her fortune into a trust so her wealth will be handed to someone closer to her."

I honestly had no idea who she would leave her fortune to in that event of her death. Knowing her, she'd probably make generous donations to charity. I was probably in her will, but I didn't need money. Legacy was important to her, she would make her wealth mean something.

"There's no chance of me getting a dime from her. That's okay because that's not what I want."

"Then what do you want?" I asked coldly.

She held my gaze, her lips pressed tightly together. For a woman in her fifties, she'd aged phenomenally well. Her skin was still beautiful, and the wrinkles around her eyes were nonexistent. She had a nice figure as well. "I want a relationship with her."

"Why?" I demanded. "You left her twenty-five years ago."

"Yes…and I shouldn't have done that."

"But you did," I snapped. "You left her. She and her father struggled every single day until he died. Then she was homeless. And after that, she built herself up and became the ruler she is now. She did that on her own—without you. Now you get to come in and have a relationship with the most amazing woman in the world?" I didn't know where all this rage came from. Now that I was face-to-face with the woman who'd abandoned my best friend, I got angry.

"I'm not going to make excuses for what I did…"

"Good. Save us both some time."

"But that doesn't change how I feel. I want to get to know her…to talk to her."

"You don't have the right." Titan was exceptionally picky about the people she allowed into her life. They had to build her trust for years before she let her guard down. This woman had already broken her trust—and she only had one shot. "Take my advice and just drop it. If you're looking for forgiveness, she's already given it to you. She doesn't hate you for the decision you made. But don't expect her to welcome you back with welcome arms. Let this go."

She looked down in shame. "I have to try."

"Don't waste your time."

"Knowing she almost died changed everything, Mr. Cutler. I understand she wants nothing to do with me, but now that I've almost lost her…I have to try. She needs to hear my apology. She needs to know I would take it back if I could."

This woman wasn't getting it. "No, she doesn't. She's fine, Bridget. She doesn't need to hear your apology to be happy. This is entirely selfish. Let it go."

"She says she doesn't need me, but I don't believe that. She lost her father, and I'm all she has left."

I wanted to slam my hand against the desk. "She has me—and she always will. I'm her family. Diesel is her family. You're just some woman who ran off. You gave her birth to her, but that's the only credit you get."

"I'm her—"

"Get out, Mrs. Creed. Go back to your husband and your two sons."

Surprise moved into her eyes. She obviously didn't expect me to know that.

"You have your own family now. Leave this in the past…where it belongs."

———

I called Autumn when I got home.

No answer.

I texted her. *Come over for dinner tonight.*

No response.

Something told me she was aware of the messages but chose to ignore me. Something in my gut told me she was upset with me. All these instincts were kicking in, but I didn't understand where they were coming from.

*Baby, please. Don't shut me out.*

Still nothing.

I didn't want to cross the line and just show up on her doorstep. Shit like that was creepy and a violation of her privacy. When women stopped by my place unexpectedly, it always ticked me off. I usually had a date over.

I texted her again. *If you change your mind, come by. I'll be waiting for you.* I tossed the phone on the table and forced myself not to stare at the screen. We weren't in a relationship, so I had no right to do anything more than wait.

She wasn't mine.

I grabbed a beer and watched the game, doing whatever I could not to think about her.

———

It was almost nine when the elevator beeped.

I jumped off the couch and staggered through the living room as I headed to the door. I hoped it was Autumn, and I assumed she was the only person it could be. Titan would just come up, and no one else would stop by randomly at this time. I hit the intercom. "Baby?"

"It's me," she said simply. "Want to buzz me in?"

I rested my forehead against the wall and smiled, relieved this was really happening. "I'd love to." I hit the button so she could rise to the top. I waited in front of the door, grateful she was coming. Autumn was about to step into my life again. I didn't feel the pain of her slipping away anymore.

The doors opened and she stepped inside, wearing black skinny jeans with tall boots. A thick green jacket covered her body, large buttons down the middle. Her dark hair was in curls, and it framed her face perfectly.

She was gorgeous.

"Hey." Now that I was face-to-face with her, I was at a loss for words. I finally had her attention, and I couldn't think of anything better to say. All my anxiousness died away now that she was in my penthouse. She wouldn't be there unless she wanted to be there. My arms circled her waist, and I leaned in to kiss her.

Like a spooked horse, she stepped away and slid out of my embrace. She turned her cheek to avoid my kiss.

She might as well have kicked me in the balls. "I think we should talk."

Fuck, she was dumping me.

"This has gotten too messy. In the beginning, it was supposed to just be a fling. Now there's talk of marriage, and then you're grabbing my thigh under the table in front of my new business partner..."

I didn't want to lose her. I hadn't had her that long, and now she was already slipping away. Our time was too short, and I wasn't ready to walk away. It'd been over a month, longer than most of my arrangements, but this seemed exceptionally short. "Then let's go back to being a fling. I'll only be professional in front of Titan and Diesel. You have my word. So, problem solved."

She crossed her arms over her chest and looked at the ground instead of me.

Wasn't that what she wanted to hear? "What else? You want to start seeing other people again?" I didn't want to do that—at all. But if that's what she wanted, then fine. I'd settle.

"No." She looked up, the same dead look on her face. "I don't want that. That's the whole problem."

Now I was lost. "Sorry?"

"It's obvious we both want completely different things."

"That's not possible. I want whatever you want, Autumn. Tell me what you want, and I'll give it to you."

She released a chuckle, but it was full of so much sorrow I actually felt the pain seep into my skin. "Thorn, you're such a brilliant man but so damn stupid."

"Excuse me?"

The smile on her face was completely sarcastic, but the emotion in her eyes was sincere. "When I first made a move on you, I told myself I could do a fling. I knew you would just break my heart, so I had to keep it light. And then we started seeing each other more, and I convinced myself everything would be alright… It's not alright. Before I even met you, I had such a crush on you. Every time I'd see you on the news or in a magazine I'd get those butterflies in my stomach. Then I met you in person…and you were even better than through the pages of a magazine."

I listened to all of it without breathing, finding the information absolutely shocking. She hid her interest in me so well. I thought she was indifferent to me most of the time.

"I got so jealous over Titan… It would happen all the time. Anytime she was mentioned, I felt a rock form in my stomach. That was the biggest sign I needed to walk away, but I didn't. You said you wanted to be exclusive, and I should have left then too...but I didn't. And now you're proposing an idea of a convenient marriage...and like an idiot, I actually want to consider it. So, this is it for me, Thorn. With every passing day, I become more emotionally attached to you. If I don't walk away now, I'm going to get crushed. So this has to end now." She took a deep breath when she finished because she'd been talking a million miles an hour up to that point. "I didn't think I'd be able to recover from my last heartbreak, and when I did, I said I wouldn't risk it again. But here I am, doing it again...only this time is worse. "This is it for me. I want to be friends and colleagues...but that's it."

I'd had plenty of time to process what she said because she'd been talking for so long. I'd had time to prepare for the bomb she dropped on my head. But I couldn't have anticipated how much her words would hurt me. They cut into me like a dirty knife that had been sitting in the soil for decades. The wound festered immediately and made me sick. I wasn't in love with this woman, but the immense amount of pain she had just caused me made me think otherwise. She said she wanted to end things, and I wanted to tell her that I didn't accept it.

That I didn't want to let her go.

I didn't want to find someone else to bring back to my place. I didn't want to see Autumn on a regular basis and pretend she was just some woman I worked with. I'd never felt this kind of attachment to anyone. "I didn't know you felt that way…"

"I did my best to hide it. I've had flings with other guys, and that was easy. We'd just have fun. I thought you wouldn't be any different. But then you were…and I wasn't strong enough to walk away."

Now would be the right time to say something meaningful, but I couldn't think of anything. Autumn had wanted me before she even met me. My proposal tempted her because she wanted me so much. "Hear me out…"

She pulled her arms tighter around her body.

"You said you were tempted by my proposal."

"For, like, a second," she whispered.

"Why?"

She shook her head.

"Just answer me."

"Having Thorn Cutler as a husband sounds pretty nice. You're not only wealthy but respectable. You're gorgeous as sin and fun to be with. You're great in bed…the best I've ever had. You're honest and loyal…I could go on."

"So the only drawback is me seeing other women?"

She closed her eyes for a moment, as if just the suggestion hurt her. "I couldn't do that. I couldn't… know you were out with someone else. I want to pretend that I would be okay, but that would be a lie. It would eat me up inside."

If she were out with someone else, I'd feel the same way. "What if I didn't see anyone else?"

She cocked her head, her eyes squinting. "What…?"

"Would you consider my proposal if we remained monogamous? I would remain faithful to you."

She stared at me as if she didn't understand a word I'd just said. "How is that any different than a regular marriage, then?"

"I guess it's not…"

"So we would just get married for the convenience and remain faithful to each other?" she asked. "Now it sounds like an arranged marriage."

"But it would give us both what we want. We could start a family, and we could both have successful partners. I bring a lot to the table, and so do you. I'm one of the most powerful men in the business world. You're one of the biggest geniuses of our time. Together, we'd be a pretty great couple. Not to mention, I'm hot and so are you. Have any idea what our kids would look like?"

An awkward laugh escaped her lips, and she stepped back. "Convenient or not, it would be risky."

"I think it's less risky. We could have good sex all the time and raise a family."

"And what if we stop liking each other?" she asked. "Then we have kids, and we can't see other people… sounds like a nightmare."

"Not if we always stay friends and talk to each other."

She looked at the ground and chewed her bottom lip. She seemed to be seriously considering it.

Would she actually say yes?

"Thorn, I don't want that either. If I marry someone, I guess I want to marry for love. Call me old-fashioned."

"But love is the reason people get divorced. Once the passion and lust die down, what's left?"

"And that's all we have, Thorn," she countered. "Passion and lust."

"I don't agree with that." I'd wanted to fuck her the first time I saw her, but I also cared about her. I confided things to her just like a friend. "I think we have more than that. We're friends."

"Friendship isn't enough either."

"You shouldn't dismiss the power of it. A real bond can be deeper than blood." Titan was the closest person in my life, and we didn't share genetics.

She shifted her weight to the side then tucked her hair behind her ear. "My ex left me for someone else. He fell in love and knew he wanted to be with her. There wasn't a doubt in his mind. That's what I want... to meet a man who knows I'm the one."

My eyes softened.

"Maybe that's stupid and unrealistic...but it's what I want. I want to protect my happiness as much as I can, but I also don't want to settle for something that will hurt me. So I should get out of this situation now because it drowns me."

She'd rejected my offer, and now she was leaving me. She wanted me, but she refused to have me unless I offered her more. She never asked me if I'd be willing to have a deeper relationship, one full of feelings and a connection.

Because she knew I'd say no.

She knew I wouldn't change my mind.

I was a confirmed bachelor, going from woman to woman with meaningless experiences. It was good sex, but it was also easy sex. I was incapable of feeling anything more than that. I did have stronger feelings for Autumn than I did for anyone else, but that was the extent of it. "I understand."

She looked away, unable to mask her disappointment. She couldn't hide her anguish.

Maybe she did hope I'd change my mind.

She cleared her throat slightly then plastered on a look of indifference. "I hope we can part of good terms."

"Of course."

"Great. I guess I should get going…" She turned toward the elevator.

I snatched her by the elbow then backed her up into the wall. I cornered her with my body, my face pressed to hers. "Not tonight." I rubbed my nose against hers then kissed the corner of her mouth. "Not until morning."

Her beautiful eyes looked into mine, the sorrow and the longing evident. Her hands moved up my bare chest, and her warm breaths fell on my face. She'd given me that look dozens of times, and I knew exactly what it meant. She wanted me. She wanted me deep, hard, and long. "Until morning."

———

Since it was my final night with this incredible woman, I could have done something more erotic and scandalous, like tying her to my headboard and fucking her from behind. I could have blindfolded her and forced her to rely on her other senses to enjoy me.

But I didn't.

I had her on her back, her legs spread for me. Her head lay on my pillow with her hair fanned out across the crumpled sheets. Her tits were firm and her nipples were peaked. Her mouth was constantly open from the all the moaning she did. She took in my length like a pro, making my dick glide through her slickness.

My wrists were locked behind her knees, keeping her wide open for me. I fucked her at a rhythmic pace, going neither slow or fast. All I wanted to do was make it last. I wanted to stay just like this, as long as she could handle me without getting sore.

"Thorn…I love it when you fuck me."

I paused as I was buried deep inside her, forcing my dick to behave itself. "Baby, I do too." I moved my mouth to hers to kiss her, keeping myself distracted so I wouldn't blow my load sooner than I wanted to. I'd already come in her once and got hard again almost instantly, but it was unlikely I could spring back so quickly.

But the kiss just made me harder.

I loved her small tongue, the way her mouth breathed into mine when she kissed me. Her mouth quivered as it danced with mine. She panted and moaned directly into my mouth, writhing underneath me like this was the very first time.

Her nails cut into my back as she held on to me. Her pussy tightened around me as she slid into another orgasm. She clenched me with bruising force and locked her ankles around my waist. Then she came loudly, sheathing my cock with all her cream. "Thorn..."

I pounded into her viciously, unable to control my thrusts. I wanted to drive my dick deep inside and give her even more of my come. She wouldn't be able to walk out of there without feeling my come sitting at her entrance, no matter how many times she showered.

She pushed her palm against the headboard so she could thrust back at me with the same force. Sweat dripped, and our moans collided. "Come inside me..." She looked beautiful just like that, fucking me back with the same vigor I showed her. She wanted me to get off with the same enthusiasm that I just had.

She wanted to rock my world.

I came inside her again with a deep moan, feeling the immediate satisfaction as I filled her gorgeous pussy with a mound of my come. I clenched my jaw as I kept going, giving her a load just as big as the previous one. All the muscles in my body tightened in pleasure. I'd never gotten off so hard to someone else in my life.

I moved on top of her and smothered her with kisses as my dick slowly softened. The come dripped onto the sheets because there was too much to fit inside her small little slit. Sex filled the room, and it would take weeks for the scent to fade away.

Not that I wanted it to.

I turned over and lay beside her, my chest covered in a thin film of sweat. The muscles of my core were tight from the exertion, but the fatigue never felt so good. Despite the heat that seared our skin, I hooked my arm around her and pulled her into me. I wanted to enjoy her as much as I could, treasure her even when I wasn't inside her. "Tell me something about yourself." I found myself missing these conversations already. We didn't always talk about anything deep and meaningful, but we did have discussions.

"About me?" she whispered.

"Yeah."

"I'm not that interesting."

"Tell me something boring about yourself, then," I teased.

"I didn't say I was boring either."

"Come on." I pressed a kiss to her forehead.

She smiled in response. "I love horses."

"Yeah? I didn't take you as a country girl."

"I wouldn't call me a country girl. But I've always wanted to have some land for a few horses."

"Do you know anything about horses?"

"Of course. When I was young, I used to work in a stable. It paid shit and I was always covered in shit, but I got to groom and train the horses. I had to take the train when I was teenager really early in the morning during the summer. But I enjoyed it."

"You know how to ride?"

"I did. It's been a while now."

"Why don't you move out to the countryside like your parents?"

"It's not convenient right now," she answered. "I'm already working so much, and adding another hour to commute each way…that'd be a pain. Maybe when I get to a place in my career when I'm not working as much, it'll be different."

"I hope that's not when you're retired."

"I hope so too," she said with a chuckle. "I've always imagined I would raise my kids outside the city. Whenever we want to do some shopping or sightseeing, we can just take the train in. But for the rest of the time, we can enjoy some fresh air."

"Yeah, that sounds nice."

"Do you always want to live in the city?"

"Honestly, I can't picture myself living anywhere else." I'd always lived in a big city my whole life. Chicago was a big city too. Not as big as Manhattan, but just as chaotic. "I like Chicago, but New York is a lot more interesting to me."

"And less windy, right?"

I smiled. "Yeah…less windy."

"Do you think you'll ever move back there? Because of your family?"

"No," I said immediately. "I prefer Manhattan. I know my brother wants to come here too. Once he does, I'm sure my parents will follow us. They're only there because that's where their house is. It's been in the family for over a hundred years, so they can't give it up."

"Over a hundred years?"

"Yeah, it's an old house with land outside the city."

"That's cool."

My hand slid through her damp hair, the sweat accumulating at her roots. When she was worn out and fatigued was when she looked the best. I liked making her lips swollen with my mouth. I loved the way she looked thoroughly fucked—by me. "How do you like working with Titan?"

"It's too soon to tell. But I'm enjoying the experience so far. She's a smart woman, and not to mention, strong as hell. I don't think I'd be back at work only six weeks after being shot."

"You're right. But that woman is made of stronger stuff than most of us."

"True."

"But I suspect you're made from the same foundation. You're a badass woman too."

"Badass?" she asked with a smile.

"Hell yeah." I rubbed my nose against hers. "I haven't met a beautiful brainiac before."

"Uh, Titan?"

"She's smart, but not a genius like you. I saw the formulas written on your whiteboard in your office. Have no idea what any of that even means."

"It's just equations."

"But there weren't any numbers. Just symbols and nonsense…"

She laughed. "That nonsense is the basis of the science."

"Well, Titan and I couldn't decode it if our lives depended on it."

"If someone taught you, I'm sure they could. Don't sell yourself short. A lot of people think science and math are too hard, but once you give it a chance, you realize it's actually mostly common sense."

I scoffed because it was ridiculous. "Maybe you just think it's easy because you're a genius."

She gave me a playful slap. "Stop calling me that."

"What? Ye."

"You're a billionaire. You don't think that qualifies you as a genius?"

"Hardly. I was born into wealth. I'm a lucky bastard. Titan, on the other hand, did everything on her own. Now that takes real talent."

Her hands glided up my chest. "Well, I heard you're the one who gave her a loan when the banks refused to take a chance on her."

My eyes narrowed. "How did you know that?"

"She told me…

She also told me she wouldn't be where she is now without you, that you pulled her up on her feet and guided the way."

I didn't realize Titan had told her that. "She exaggerates."

"We both know that's bullshit." She smiled at me, knowing she had me backed into a corner. "You invested in her because you knew she'd make you a fortune. And you were right. You know what that makes you?"

"Don't say it—"

"A sexy genius."

Before I could get angry, I focused on the first word she said. "Sexy, huh?"

"Don't act like you aren't one of the sexiest guys in the world."

"I'm not ignorant to my charms, but one of the sexiest…that's a pretty flattering statement."

"And I mean it." She rubbed my chest then kissed me.

Oh wow. I loved her kisses.

She kissed me slowly like we hadn't been fucking all night. There was tongue, lots of lip, and the sexiest moans.

My hand explored her body again, feeling her tight stomach and her awesome tits. It took less than a minute for my dick to come to full mast again. Then I rolled her over, knowing exactly how I wanted to take her, be buried between her legs while she was pinned underneath me.

I didn't want to sleep.

I just wanted to move with her.

Talk to her.

And move with her again.

———

My alarm went off with a shriek. It was the most unpleasant sound I'd ever heard, but it had never bothered me any other morning.

Only today, it was unwelcome.

My blissful night was officially a memory. It was something of the past, something to look back on. Now I would move on with my life. She would move on with hers.

She got out of bed first, her movements slower than usual. She pulled on her panties first then took her time with her bra. Each piece of clothing was slowly draped across her gorgeous skin.

I wanted to make love to her again, but I knew it wouldn't feel good.

It would just be depressing.

I got out of bed and pulled on a fresh pair of boxers.

She zipped up her boots then arranged her hair with her fingers. Since the alarm went off, she hadn't looked at me.

I didn't make eye contact with her either.

She finally walked to the door, dressed in her green jacket and ready to go.

I followed her to the entryway.

Last night, it felt so right. Despite the fact that it was our last night together, it felt so comfortable. It was simple. But now, it was the tensest interaction we'd ever had. It was stiff, as if we hardly knew each other at all.

She grabbed her purse off the table then immediately hit the button for the elevator.

She was trying to get out of there as quickly as possible.

I could just let her go without a fight to make it easier on both of us, but it felt insulting to watch her walk out with a single glance. I grabbed her arm and guided her into my chest, my arms wrapping around her like steel bars.

Her face rested against my chest.

I didn't know what to say to make this blow easier for either of us. She admitted she was falling for me, and I admitted I cared about her more than I should. We were cutting this off before it could grow into something real. We were burning the wound shut before it could bleed. I pressed a kiss to her hairline and smelled her scent one last time. I'd probably never be this close to her ever again.

She took a breath, like she was appreciating me as much as I was appreciating her.

The elevator beeped when the doors opened.

She rose on her tiptoes and gave me a kiss, a soft one on the mouth. There was no heat or passion like there was last night. There was only a sorrowful good-bye. She turned away, her hand dragging down my chest until she was inside the elevator.

I stared as she turned around and met my gaze.

The doors closed.

And I watched her disappear from my sight.

The doors shut, a metal obstacle separating us permanently.

Now she was gone.

I would never see her again...see her the way I liked to see her.

# CHAPTER TWELVE

TITAN

"Diesel, you don't need to come." I folded my clothes and placed them in the suitcase on the bed.

He moved behind me, packing things for the trip. "I'm aware."

"I'm serious." I kept my eyes on my suitcase. Staring at him was always too much of a distraction. "We don't need to do everything together just because we're getting married."

"I'm aware of that too." His heavy footsteps shuffled behind him as he moved.

I rolled my eyes. "Then stay here. I'm just going to be working the whole time."

He came to my side, his shadow stretching over me. He suspended a sparkly piece of lingerie in front of me then dropped it on top of the rest of my clothing. The panties and bra came with it, made with real diamonds.

I immediately wanted to squeeze my thighs together.

Diesel moved in closer to me, his lips coming next to my ear. "And when you aren't working, you'll be fucking." He kissed the shell of my ear before he turned away and walked to his closet.

Goose bumps formed on my arms even though he'd turned me on so many times. I touched the sparkling lingerie then carefully folded it before placing it on top of the rest of my clothes. "I can always wear this when I get back."

"Where you go, I go."

I rolled my eyes again even though he couldn't see me. "When you go on business trips, don't expect me to come along."

"You will be coming along," he said coldly. "And your suitcase will be full of only lingerie."

A smile formed on my lips.

He couldn't see my face, but he predicted my reaction. "I'm being serious."

"I know," I whispered. "That's why I'm smiling."

He shut his suitcase then set it by the door. "Anyone coming along?"

"Autumn and Thorn are joining us."

He sighed loudly, which told me it was on purpose. "What?"

"I don't like to share you."

"A few hours on a plane is too much for you?" I asked sarcastically.

"Yes. A single hour is too much." He was in jeans and a black t-shirt. He looked amazing in dark colors. It added to his quiet aggressiveness. He came to my side at the bed and stared at me openly, possessing me with a single look.

"Last chance to back out…" We had to leave in the next fifteen minutes. I set my bag of makeup on top along with a brush and some hairspray.

"I'm not backing out. Having me by your side only increases your power. I've seen the way people talk to you sometimes. People won't say a damn thing to you while I'm there."

It was sweet, but not to me. "I don't need you to make my problems go away. I've established my power on my own, and I don't need a guard dog to maintain it. I've earned my reputation by example, not fear. The second I hide behind a man, I forfeit that respect. So let's get that straight right now. I represent my businesses on my own. It's completely separate from you, as I'm separate from your businesses. We may be combined in every other way, but that's where we draw the line. If you think I need you to come to my rescue… then you don't know me at all." I shut my suitcase then carried it to the elevator, moving around him and ignoring him.

He came up behind me, his heavy footsteps slow. He carried his suitcase with him then set it by the door.

I knew the argument wasn't over.

He crossed his arms over his chest and stared at me as we waited in front of the elevator.

It was like waiting for a bomb to explode. Any moment now, he would snap.

I caved first. "What?"

"We're a team, in all aspects. We're joined completely. When people look at you, they think of me. Vice versa. We're the richest couple in the world now, Titan. That kind of power shouldn't be handled lightly. People are going to try to tear us down. I have your back, and you better have mine."

"You know I do."

"Then where you go is where I go. Your businesses are my businesses."

"I don't need your help running them."

"But we're a team now. I get that's gonna be a difficult adjustment for you, but you need to accept it." He stared me down with his fierce expression, obviously not happy about the attitude I just gave him.

We still hadn't spoken of the legal ramifications of our union. We'd have to talk about finances, ownerships, trusts…a bunch of difficult discussions that I was dreading. We were getting married because we loved each other, but soon we'd have to treat it like a business acquisition.

The elevator beeped, and the doors opened to reveal Thorn. Dressed in jeans and a hoodie, he had one bag over his shoulder. His hair was messy like he didn't bother styling it when he got out of the shower that morning. His eyes didn't shine with their usual excitement when we traveled places. He stepped into the penthouse without giving us more than a nod.

Something was wrong.

"Out late with Autumn?" I asked.

Thorn set his bag on the ground. "No. When are we leaving?"

Judging by his clipped tone, he didn't want to talk about Autumn. That couldn't be good. "The guys will be here any minute. But if you aren't feeling well, you don't have to come along."

"I'm feeling fine." He helped himself to the bar and made himself an Old Fashioned...even though it was nine in the morning.

Diesel dropped his hostility when he realized Thorn was losing his grip on reality. He eyed him then turned back to me, having a silent conversation with me.

I shook my head in response, unsure what to do about Thorn. The guys would be here to escort us to the airport any second, and then Autumn would join us for the flight. If there were something else on Thorn's mind, he would just blurt it out. So it was obviously about Autumn.

He downed the glass in less than a minute then came back to us, reeking of booze.

We were off to a great start...

The elevator doors opened again, and my team stepped inside to collect my things. They grabbed my bags, along with Diesel's and Thorn's, and then we went down to the lobby and boarded the black SUV waiting for us.

Diesel didn't sit beside me and moved into the very back row, assuming I would want to sit next to Thorn during the ride.

Damn, he knew me well.

Thorn sat beside me, buckled his safety belt, and then faced forward like we were two strangers on the bus. His normally good-natured expression was wiped away and replaced by a painful look of irritation.

He didn't look like himself at all.

"Thorn?"

"Hmm?"

I hit the button and raised the center divider so the guys couldn't hear us. "What happened with Autumn?"

We hit a pothole in the road, and his body swayed slightly with the movement. He kept his gaze out the window and didn't break his stare. "We aren't seeing each other anymore."

"Why?" If he was so miserable without her, why go their separate ways?

"Doesn't matter," he said quietly. "You don't need to worry about our business relationship. We're fine."

"That's not what I'm worried about." Couldn't care less about it. I'd never seen my friend looked so upset in my life. Even when I'd been shot, he didn't look this pale. He plastered a smile on his face while he sat at my bedside and played cards with me. "What happened?"

"It's a long and boring story…"

"We have time before we pick her up."

He stared out the window, ignoring me.

I grabbed his hand. "Talk to me. You know I'm just going to bug you until you open up."

He pulled his hand away. "She basically told me she couldn't have a fling anymore because she was falling for me…she wants all of me instead of some of me. I couldn't give her what she wanted, so we called it off."

It didn't surprise me Autumn wanted something more from Thorn. He was an incredible man with a heart of solid gold. He was greedy for power and extremely ambitious, but he was also compassionate about people who didn't have what he had. He helped me get to where I was now and never expected anything in return. He was extremely selfless. "If you couldn't give her what she wanted, then why are you so miserable right now?"

He didn't answer.

"Thorn, just give it a chance. What do you have to lose?"

"It's not gonna go anywhere, Titan. I'll just waste her time and hurt her in the end. She'll tell me she loves me, and I won't say it back. It'll kill her. I could never do that…not to her. She deserves something so much better than me."

"Then be what she deserves, Thorn."

He shook his head, his eyes still out the window. "I'm not gonna repeat myself."

"You wouldn't be miserable over her if you didn't care about her."

"Of course I care about her," he said quietly. "Never said I didn't."

"Then keep caring about her...everything else will come naturally."

The guys pulled over to the curb, stopping in front of Autumn's house.

"Let's drop it," Thorn whispered.

The front door opened, and she appeared with her suitcase. The guys got out to help her, and I finished what I needed to say. "Let me break this down for you, Thorn. If you let her go, someone else is gonna get her. Then you'll watch her be happy from a distance, wishing you were the guy sleeping beside her every night. Don't let that be you, Thorn. Take a risk. You have more to lose by doing nothing than by doing something."

She was almost to the SUV.

Thorn didn't say anything.

"Just think about what I said." I squeezed his hand then pulled away right when the door opened.

Autumn was dressed nicely, and her hair was done. But she held the same sadness in her eyes that Thorn did. She did a better job at hiding it, though. "Morning."

"Morning." Diesel gave her a hand and helped her inside. They sat side by side.

"Hey, Autumn," I said. "How are you?"

"Great." She buckled her safety belt. "I'm excited to see Chicago."

Thorn didn't say anything to her. He didn't turn around to look at her.

I tapped my knee against his.

Thorn cleared his throat. "Morning…Autumn." He said her name like it actually caused him pain deep in his gut. It was like he'd never really said her name before or addressed her that way.

Autumn took a long pause before she said it back. "Morning, Thorn."

I could feel the tension in the air, the sadness between them both. Neither one of them was taking this breakup well. Thorn was miserable, and she was obviously distraught too.

I wanted my best friend to have what I had, a love that had no boundaries. I'd found everything I ever needed within Diesel. He completed me in a way money and success never could. He was my partner for life, the future father of my children. Finding someone that remarkable who loved you unconditionally was worth more than all the money in the world.

And I didn't want Thorn to lose it.

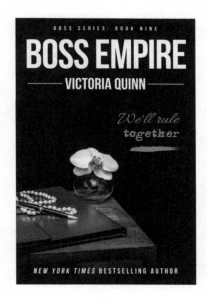

CPSIA information can be obtained
at www.ICGtesting.com
Printed in the USA
LVHW02s0044280818
588281LV00001B/208/P